D1599353

"FAULT LINE"

a collection of short fiction
by Jo-Ann Mapson

Pacific Writers Press

Cover Photo and Design: Stewart Allison

ISBN: 0-944870-02-3
Library of Congress Catalog Card Number: 89-62971

Acknowledgements

"The Red Nightie Network" won the 1986 California Short Story Competition and first appeared in *The Nob Hill Gazette.*

*

"Cakewalk" first appeared in the spring 1988 issue, volume 6, of *Elephant-Ear.* The author is grateful for permission to reprint.

*

"The Rings of Saturn" has been purchased for publication in *Orange Coast Magazine's* 1989 Christmas issue.

*

"Thirty-Second Poses," "Owning the View," "Baby Steps" and "Cakewalk" were scholarship winners in Orange Coast College's writing competitions during the period of 1985-1988.

* * *

Many thanks to Alejandro Morales and Bob Boies for taking a chance on my writing. I also offer my gratitude to those whose encouragement kept me going when it felt like all I was doing was treading the waters of rejection: Stewart and Jack Allison, Jane Bernstein, Deb Brenner, Larry Carlson, John Hermann, Richard Linder, the editors of the *Nob Hill Gazette,* Ron Stathes, the members of Fictionaires, especially Noreen Ayres, M.J. Roberts, C. R. Saunders, Robert Ray and Don Stanwood.

Contents

the first one is for Frank, as promised

Now, there is another world
under the one we live on.
You can reach it by going
down a spring, a water hole;
but you need underworld people
to be your scouts and guide you.

EARTH MAKING
Cherokee legend

INTRODUCTION TO FAULT LINE

Driving home one night from a lecture which I had given in Long Beach and which, in an act of friendship, my fellow writer Jo-Ann Mapson had offered to attend, I spoke to her about her short stories. With a great deal of sweating, agonizing, and hair-pulling, I had managed to create a single short story between the months of October and January during the previous year. Afterwards, I had occasion to read Jo-Ann's collection, FAULT LINE, for the first time. Although I had heard Jo-Ann read her work aloud before, although I had admired it when listening to it, her stories had not had the power to touch me deeply when I was merely a listener. The act of reading, however, which engenders intimacy between reader and writer, also increases writing's intensity. As a result, I found myself not only touched but dazzled again and again by Jo-Ann's work. Thus, as we drove along Pacific Coast Highway, I spoke to her about my feelings of inadequacy as a short story writer, juxtaposing this inadequacy with her own remarkable facility for examining the lives of everyday people in a manner enriched by compassion and ennobled by fellow-feeling.

Jo-Ann was surprised by my conclusion: I am a novel writer first and a short story writer only through an effort so enervating that no creation produced by such endeavor could possibly be worth the endeavor itself. I always think in terms of the big canvas, I told her. I'm incapable of seeing the inherent fascination with which small details imbue everyday life.

You're looking at it all wrong, she told me. Remember the lady you told me about in the London cemetery...the lady wearing pink rubber gloves and digging around a grave in the rain?

Yes, of course, I remembered. I'd gone to South Ealing Cemetery to look at the location for the final scene in a novel I would be writing soon afterwards. I'd made notes. I'd taken photographs. I'd walked around the quiet grounds in the rain. And I'd come upon this woman, digging, wearing bright pink rubber gloves, a raincoat, one of those accordion-like fold-up plastic rainhats. She worked industriously while nearby, her husband sat waiting in their car, reading a newspaper, smoking a cigarette. I'd made a brief note about the woman and, when I arrived at that final scene in my novel, I popped her into the cemetery next to the grave where one of my characters was being laid to rest. So I did remember her.

She's a short story, Jo-Ann explained.

Tell me, I said.

And she showed me the process through which a glimpse of a person, a detail of clothing, an expression on a face, or a snatch of conversation overheard begins to dominate her thoughts, begins to develop—in arboreal fashion—a life of its own. The roots: that first moment when she realizes that some part of her experience has the potential to be a story. The trunk: those weeks and months in which the story begins to take form in her mind. The branches: that period of time when the characters establish themselves, developing substance. The leaves: the act of creation itself.

How simple she made it sound that night. How simple it appears in this collection of stories. Using faultless imagery, an understated manipulation of our language, and an exploration of the lives of ordinary people, Jo-Ann elevates experiences that other authors might shrug off as unworthy of examination. It is not an unnatural elevation, however. Rather, it is a process of conferring dignity and grace upon areas of life where they are both deserved.

In "Statistics," for example, the nurturing of a nest-fallen baby bird is set against a mother's agonized preoccupation with her small son's health. He'd been saved as a baby through the means of transfusions, just before the AIDS scare began. So the mother faces the everyman dilemma: Is it better to know the truth or to create a fantasy in which truth may be avoided? Is it better to try to save the baby bird—knowing how unlikely it is that a bird so small could be nurtured to adulthood—or to place it carefully in the juncture of two branches of a tree and tell yourself that it will somehow survive? Does one say I'll leave my life to God or fate or destiny or karma? Or does one say I'll take risks, I'll make decisions, I'll try. It is indeed, the everyman dilemma.

In "Cake Walk," a woman fumbles through the process of helping her sister through the grief and the horror and the rage of being a victim of rape. No heroic speeches, no acts of valor. Just canned shoestring potatoes, Thrifty's vanilla ice cream, and an evening at the local county fair where a pink peppermint cake—and a moment of triumph so minor it would be forgotten in any other life—becomes the catalyst for freeing an imprisoned soul.

Small moments are magnified in FAULT LINE. Fragments of conversations take on multi-leveled significance. Although ordinary people seem to live out their lives in very ordinary ways, they do not do so without touching our own lives first. This is the very essence of fine writing.

Elizabeth George

15

THE RED NIGHTIE NETWORK

It was one of those last minute, scene-of-the-crime persuasive purchases I always seem to make at the pit of depression — for $5.99, a blood-red shortie nightgown with spaghetti straps piped in ecru lace.

I took it off the sale rack and hid it under several pair of stockings, the old-fashioned kind to use with a garter belt. I knew it was silly to resist the acquiescence to pantyhose, but something in me rebelled at that elastic clutching my stomach as if it were punishment for being born female. Gilbert's, a department store that had seen better days, was the last bastion for regular stockings like these without nurse seams or that sexy ribbing that projected an image I didn't intend. So I cleaned out the entire cubbyhole of Suntan, size A. It was a long drive and I didn't want to come back any sooner than was necessary.

Especially with my son Benjamin in tow. He was three days out of the hospital and for all I knew, three days from returning. I looked at his black eye and felt a tug at my heart. A memento from a chance meeting with a Fisher-Price xylophone. It happens to every kid. Usually the parents take a photograph and it gets lost in an album somewhere, faded pen on the back: "Ben's first shiner." But because Ben's blood lacked a certain clotting factor, he needed transfusions to control the bleeding that would not stop of its own accord, not even beneath the surface. I didn't need pictures.

He kept dragging his feet under the stroller. He was bored, too old to be confined. I didn't blame him. I hurried to finish my shopping. It felt as if people were staring: did they think I was some kind of terrible mother, hog-tying a four-year-old (with a

17

black eye, no less) down like that? The unspoken insinuations made me feel guilty. But every mundane outing without the stroller turned into a risk. Just as tentative a risk as letting him run into a group of unfamiliar children had been. How was I to know they were miniature guerrillas, armed with xylophones? Deep down I knew it could have just as easily been a bump into playground equipment or a friendly punch from a five-year-old establishing territorial limits. I couldn't keep him in a plastic bubble like that kid I read about in the newspaper.

The clerk wrapped the nightgown in tissue paper. She was overweight, shapeless, dressed in colors as muted and forgettable as the birds that gathered on the lawn of the hospital before dawn. I had monitored their behavior in the early morning hours when there is nothing to do in the children's ward except drink a cup of tepid coffee, be glad the needles have been inserted properly and the hours are progressing toward a new day. She handed me the brown paper bag as if it held something of importance, something very precious. I suppressed an urge to laugh. Maybe she applauded my protest of the garment industry's attempt to put us all in tights. Or maybe she had her own ideas of what just such a nightgown might accomplish. I pushed Ben through the parking lot, mindful that his dragging feet did not catch on the curbing.

* * *

At first I thought I would keep it secret from both Belinda and Dorie, though I told them nearly everything else. Belinda was the closest thing to a best friend I had. She lived three houses down and one across, with her fanatical runner husband and a five-year-old daughter with asthma. We commiserated daily over too much coffee, taking each other into caffeine confidences.

I thought to myself as I folded the nightgown (it was so light, it felt like nothing but a slight itch in my hand) into my underwear drawer: Belinda will never understand this. Belinda of the flannel granny gowns that have lasted her since high school. She'll tell

Dave, who will in turn tell my husband as they click off their requisite miles around the track. And then it will be neutralized, an eyesore, something I will be embarrassed about each time I see that shade of red. She'll give me a look and I'll know that I'm too old for this silliness.

So I told Dorie. Who I didn't know very well. Whose son, young Kevin, not to be confused with her husband, old Kevin, has cystic fibrosis.

It was the kind of thing we found laughable after several glasses of wine — three women living so close in proximity, managing to find themselves in roughly the same position. Was it the water we drank?

"Sometimes I feel like I'm raising a dying child," Dorie said to me.

I poured her a cup of coffee and added real cream. I knew it was something she loved, a little homey touch she never would have given herself. She talked.

"Belinda says 'come over and we'll make personalized Christmas ornaments for the kids.' I just want to scream. Sooner or later there's going to be a Christmas when young Kevin won't be among us. It's a given. What'll I do with a miniature sled with his name stencilled on it then?"

She lit a cigarette and sighed, cupping it in her palm like I had done back in high school, when the illicitness of the act provided more pleasure than the actual smoking.

"You don't know what it's like, Nance. This is my last vice. You're not supposed to smoke around CF patients. I'm thinking of asking old Kevin to build me a backyard greenhouse. I could tell him I've always wanted to raise orchids just so I can have a place to sneak my coffin nails. Probably kill the plants. Or with my luck, they'll thrive, the bastards."

Her shoulders shook with laughter, but I knew that kind of laughter too well. One false move and it would end up as tears. "Wait right there," I told her. "I have something to show you. It'll cheer you up." I fetched the red nightie and unfolded it, dangling it in front of my body.

19

She set her cigarette down in the saucer of her cup. "Let me see that." Fanning herself as if the nightgown was a source of intense heat, she flashed me a rare smile. "Jesus," she said. "What do you think? Am I having my first hot flash?"

I smiled back. "Isn't it lucky I was here to share it with you?"

At thirty-four, she still possessed that leanness I had left behind at sixteen. She was dark, olive-skinned to Belinda's blondeness. Belinda was wholesome-pretty. Natural. I thought if we were lined up, Dorie would be singled out as the most attractive. I was mouse; neither color was quite my camp.

"I'm a little embarrassed. It's not the sort of thing I usually buy. It just sort of ran out from the sale rack, jumped into my purse, found the charge card and paid for itself."

"Don't apologize," Dorie said, fingering the lace and poking the bra cups so that they stood out obscenely. "This is the best laugh I've had in weeks."

I took it from her and crumpled it in my palm, intending to take it back to the bedroom and bury it.

"God," she said. "You're so sensitive. Bring it back. I was only teasing." She held it up so that it caught light from the lamp on my desk. The steam from her coffee cup trailed behind it like it was smoking hot.

"What do you really think?" I asked her. "Truthfully."

"We're not that different in the jahoobie department. I wonder if it would fit me?"

Before I could say anything, she trotted off to the bathroom to give it a try.

* * *

She returned it a few days later, laundered, aromatic of Final Touch, along with a bottle of zinfandel tied in a blood-red ribbon. Belinda just happened to knock at the door to borrow a cup of honey at the same time. I held the wine in one hand, the nightgown in the other. Caught.

She set her plastic measuring cups in a stack on the table.

They looked like Ben's toy that was supposed to demonstrate spatial relationships. "What's going on, ladies? Anything you'd care to share?"

"A change of pace," Dorie told her. "Here's the ticket." She unfolded my nightie. Belinda's eyes bulged.

"I was going to make a spice cake," she said, whistling. "Carbo-packing for the big race, you know. Anything to get Dave's mind off splits and adequate heel support. Maybe I'll try this instead." She tucked it inside the one-cup measure and we all laughed. "Except it probably won't work. He thinks pre-race sex takes valuable minutes off his time."

Dorie reached for her cigarettes. "It does. What does it take, Nance? Fifty minutes?"

I scoffed. "What are you doing, bragging? Maybe fifteen at the outside."

We were all silent for a minute, awkward in the kitchen under the overhead fixtures. It lacked something that would have made it a really comfortable place to gather. Another window. More direct sunlight. Something.

Dorie smoked quickly, pulling on the cigarette like there was a promise of something better at the other end. "Young Kevin has clinic this afternoon," she explained. "I have to smoke twice as much now so I won't have a fit later."

Belinda shuddered. "Don't remind me of clinic. Mandy had a bad night. We took her to the ER about 2:30 this morning."

She crossed her arms and the nightgown slipped out of the cup and spilled onto the floor. It lay there for a moment before she noticed, just so much nylon and chintz.

"Did she have to be admitted?" Dorie asked.

Belinda, her mouth full of coffee, shook her head no.

"What brought it on this time?" I wanted to know.

Belinda smiled, earth-mother, the all-accepting smile I had a suspicion was really an affectation of too little sleep. "Guys," she said. "She's fine. Dave found a whole pile of candy wrappers behind her bed. Guilt-induced asthma. *Voila.*"

Secretly, I thought Mandy was a spoiled brat. Sure, I felt for

21

for her, denied the chocolate she craved on her maintenance medicine. But she was such an impossible child. Hostile, almost. Once I had tried to cheer her with some scented stickers. Blueberry, lemonade, chocolate among them. Mandy ate all the chocolate ones and threw up on my carpet. Belinda said she'd tried baking goodies with carob. But wise Mandy knew the difference and would have none of that.

"Where's Ben?" Belinda asked me. "I haven't seen him out playing. Is he okay?"

That was the phrase we handed back and forth rather than come right out and ask, fearful of the answer. It was the stance we struck around doctors who spoke tersely, giving odds rather than admit uncertainty.

"On a scale of one to ten, give him a six," I said, leading them through the kitchen to the playroom, opening doors old Kevin had helped to install the previous weekend.

The television pumped out cartoons. One of my favorites: the little owlet confronting his choices. He can sing *Drink to Me Only With Thine Eyes* and please his father or follow his heart and sing jazz: *I Love to Sing-a, About the Moon-a* and the *June-a and the Spring-a*.

Ben lay on his back, his left leg swaddled in Ace bandages.

"Good God," Dorie said. "What did he do?"

"Peanut butter jar on the instep," I said, thinking back on how he was impatient, wanting lunch immediately and I had made him wait. "The doctor doesn't want him to move his ankle for two weeks."

"Good for the doctor," Dorie said. "Let him babysit."

"He's worried about the possibility of rebleeding." I made my voice sound casual, but as always, discussing the event after it happened sent me careening to that place where it seemed I was gripping my intestines to keep from falling over.

Belinda touched my shoulder. Her eyes were pure Bambi's mother, just prior to the forest fire. "I feel so bad for you, Nance."

"Why feel for her?" Dorie said. "He's the one tied up."

22

"It's the blood. There's something about the idea of blood. I just don't think I could handle it."

Dorie and I watched her crossing the street back toward her house, carrying the cupful of nightgown. We sat back down at the kitchen table.

"I wish you hadn't lent her that nightie. It makes me sick inside when I think about Mother Nature wearing it. She'll probably rub safflower oil on her tits before she puts it on."

I laughed. "Did I have a choice? You offered it to her." I let her chew on that while I went to check on Ben.

He was playing with his fire trucks, driving them up his bandaged leg and screeching to a halt at the safety pin. Sky of blue, tea for two, the little owl was singing.

I sat down next to him, moving his Super Hero dominoes aside. "How's the foot? Uncomfortable?"

"No. When do I get my next pill?"

"You fibber. It does hurt."

He ran the fire truck up my arm. "No. But I like those pills."

"Why? I have to crush them in strawberry jelly so you can swallow them."

"'Cause then I can go to sleep," he said. "It's like flying." He continued putt-putting along my arm, turning at my shoulder. I reached up and stopped him from driving down my breast.

"Then you don't really need one. Let's go to the bathroom."

"No! I don't have to go." He rolled out of my reach.

"Suit yourself," I said and left the door to the playroom ajar behind me.

Dorie was running a pencil across the margin of my *Times* crossword puzzle, making smudges. "Belinda's a suck," she said.

As long as it wasn't me she was flaying, I enjoyed her vocabulary. "I give up. Why is she a suck?"

"All that crap about blood. Hell, I'm glad my kid doesn't have a fucking psychosomatic illness like asthma. At least with CF I know where I stand."

I stirred the sugar bowl for something to do with my hands. "That's bullshit. Asthma's a trip to Hawaii compared to CF."

"I swear. I'm serious."

"But there's hope with asthma. The possibility things might change for the better."

For all her curses and invocations, she was quiet.

I thought while I made sand dunes inside the sugar bowl. The little owlet in the cartoons finally receives his father's blessing to sing jazz after he wins a talent search. At four, Ben already understood that a pill would deliver him from boredom to sleep. Belinda, the suck, had my red nightie.

"Hope," Dorie said and crumpled her empty cigarette pack, tossing it onto the table between us. "Now there is a strange concept for you."

* * *

Ben was asleep on the fold-out couch, one hand clutching his groin. His bandaged leg stuck out like an elephant's trunk. I picked him up and carried him to the bathroom. He woke up for a moment, wobbling before me, staring with unfocused eyes while he urinated.

"See? You did have to go."

"Sing," he said, and fell back to sleep.

I lay him in the tangle of sheets and smoothed the hair from his face.

* * *

The next time I held the nightgown in my hands it smelled like Belinda's Ph-balanced soap from Shaklee. Maybe it was Amway. I knew it was supposed to be good for the environment, but it didn't do much for the red nightie. I rinsed it out under the bathroom tap and let it dry in the shower stall.

My husband did stretching exercises before he went to bed. He was going to run a 10K with old Kevin and Dave in the morning and I could sense his anxiety. I had done my part, feeding him a proper pre-race dinner of pasta. It seemed logical he would relax in my arms. But he slept curled away from me in the double bed, sleep claiming him as soon as his head hit the pillow. I lay awake for a long time and listened for the sound of his breathing, then for Ben's, a miniature echo in the dark. I thought of that nightgown dripping, the action it had already seen while I explored the territory between sleep and dreaming. I wondered if it would do for me what it had done for my friends.

* * *

Unwrapping Ben's leg, running the washcloth over the dimpled skin, I noticed the bruise had spread, dark as a plum in places. He lay back against his pillows, one arm clutching a stuffed seal while his free hand worked an armless Chewbacca.

"Let's soak your foot in some water," I said.

"No."

I knew he didn't want me touching it, but the blue-green toes and puffy arch were beginning to smell tart. "Come on, Ben. Give me a break."

"No." It seemed like his favorite word.

"Your foot's sore again, isn't it? We'll ask the doctor to take another look at it."

His shoulders slumped a little.

I held the bowl of water I'd brought to wash him with and sat down next to him. "You know I'm sorry. If I could I'd take the pain away from you like that." I snapped my fingers.

He pushed the seal into my chest and broke into angry tears. "I hate," he said and upturned the bowl of water deliberately.

I let the wetness spread and did nothing. "What do you hate?" I asked. "Tell me."

"Blood!" he screeched, his voice winding high in fury.

It made me cringe to hear that sound come out of him. He tried his hardest to pull away from my arms, but I held him anyway. His anger no match for my hope.

* * *

25

Belinda sat next to me at clinic. There were so few bleeders they teamed us up with the asthmatics. It meant we could share a ride.

Mandy went from corner to corner of the isolation waiting room and picked up toys, letting them drop from her hands onto the linoleum with a loud crack. It irritated me. I needed a little peace and quiet before Ben and I faced the resident who had drawn the lucky job of draining the clot on his foot. It was an old method, rarely used, but it might halt the swelling.

Ben sat in his stroller, feigning disinterest in Mandy's progress. I watched his eyes track her across the room and dart down when she looked at him.

"Do you want me to push you to the puzzle table?"

"No."

I smiled. "Okay."

He pointed and I pushed the stroller over. He put his hands into the box. I set the brake and went back to the couch where Belinda sat crocheting something out of undyed wool that smelled strongly of sheep.

"Dorie called me this morning," she said. "Among other things, she wanted to trade red nightie stories."

I laughed.

"Why's that so funny?"

"It's not. It's just so Dorie."

"It's none of her business."

"I'm sure she meant nothing personal by it."

"Well, just between you and me," Belinda said, "I think if any of us ever split up, it'll be her and old Kevin." Her fingers loosened a knot in the yarn. "She's so sarcastic. As if she's trying to prove something."

"Aren't we all?" I asked, keeping my eyes on the children.

Mandy crossed the room and tried to take a puzzle piece from Ben. She let his arm drop when he resisted, as if she didn't want it after all. Then as soon as he found an interlocking piece of blue sky, she bent and took a bite of his forearm. I ran to him, watching the indentations in his skin go from dead white meat to

26

purple as they suffused with blood. He was crying that soundless cry that takes the breath away. I stood there for a moment, unsure what to do first. "Ice," I called to a girl at the nurse's station. "Get some ice."

Belinda bent down and took Mandy by the upper arms as if to shake her, then spoke in a pastoral voice. "We don't bite. Biting is what animals do because they don't have words. Not humans."

Mandy did this dance-away stare, focused on some place in the room that no one could ever hope to pin-point, her straggly braids trailing over her shoulders.

"Belinda?" I said, slopping ice into Ben's lap, my teeth feeling too big, as if they were tapping against each other in my mouth. "Can't you just for once beat the shit out of that kid when she deserves it?"

"It's the medication," Belinda said. "Not her." She took Mandy by the hand and left the room.

* * *

Dorie entered the house without knocking, startling me for a moment. She had been crying and was trying to light a cigarette with a tired old match that wouldn't cooperate.

"Wine," she said, as if it were a password.

"The dregs of the zinfandel," I said. "That's all I have."

"Fine." She yanked a clean coffee cup from the rack above the stove. I filled it.

"Is young Kevin okay?"

"Yeah. I dumped him on my mother. She says, 'Be back in two hours. You know I get nervous.' Jesus. What does she think I get? No one wants to babysit any more. And old Kevin is either running like a goddamn jack rabbit or knocking holes in the walls." She mimicked his voice. "Hon, I think a staircase'd be real nice here. Wham." She drank her wine in gulps. "I feel like a secret agent, rushing over here with my neuroses hidden under my trench coat." She laughed, exposing long white teeth that were normally disguised by her set expression of determination.

At that moment, I knew Dorie as well as I ever wanted to. If her friendship were a door you could choose to open or not, I knew I would have passed right by, feeling uneasy at the vibrations emanating from the grain itself.

"At least your mother's honest," I said. "You ought to hear mine. In every letter, it's 'when are you going to have another baby?'"

"You're kidding. She still won't acknowledge the fact that you had the tubal?"

"No. And I offered to send her a picture of my scar and everything."

"Sounds generous."

"I thought so. Apparently she didn't. But Dorie. What happened?"

"Just another CF funeral. For the little girl who moved here from England." She circled her hand around the coffee cup. "For the climate," she said, and tears started falling across the placemat in front of her, trickling down her arm as she leaned against it.

"You've been to a lot of funerals. But I've never seen you cry."

She looked at me as surprised as Belinda had the day she'd caught me with the nightgown. "When it comes right down to it, you can blame nearly all injustice on a supreme lack of babysitters. I took young Kevin with me. It was up on Harbor Ridge. This gorgeous hill with a view of the water. He turns to me and says, 'Mom, I want to live here forever!' Like it's somebody's dream house lot. Not a fucking graveyard."

I put a hand on her shoulder and felt the tension humming inside her. If I asked her how she could stand it, I was a suck like Belinda. I wanted to give her something, even if it were only one of Ben's pills. I didn't say anything, but that didn't fool her.

She looked into my face. "You tell me. Is there an alternative?"

28

* * *

Now there were two inch-long incisions I had to attend to.
Ben's foot was almost back to normal, but the doctor had filled
me so full of paranoia about infection that I took the dressing
changes very seriously. A nurse had shown me how to maintain
sterile procedure. Bulky white packets with disposable suture
removal kits lined the medicine cabinet. I could, if I did it properly, use a clean pair of tweezers to lift the soaked gauze and never
once touch his skin.

"How are you doing, sport?"

He pointed to the bowl of bandages stained the burnt-orange
of the Betadine antiseptic. "It's yucky, isn't it?"

"Oh, I've seen worse."

"Really?" He was all sparkly, interested in anything more
gory than his own foot. It made my throat nearly close up when
he smiled like that.

"Sure. Once I watched your grandpa's horse have a baby.
Talk about gross."

"Tell me again where that grandpa is, Mom."

"Heaven," I said, trying to make my face bright, the words
simple and natural. I was getting pretty good at the bandages. I
unwrapped new gauze and spread ointment on a swab without
even touching the cotton tip. I thought about my father, who had
died long before I considered having children. He was a down-
home fellow who thought nothing of breaking the neck of a
deformed newborn pup while I watched. A man who would stay
up all night talking his favorite mare through a difficult labor.

Ben wriggled his toes in brief freedom. "Do they have cartoons in heaven?"

"They'd better." I taped the corners of the bandage and
gathered the dirty instruments into a towel. "Do you want
anything? Batman? Comics? A peanut butter sandwich?"

He ran his hand over the clean bandage. "Can you find me
cartoons?"

I could. I did. His face broke into a grin at the sight of Tom and Jerry running across the screen. He settled his stuffed animals around him like chessmen. I knew enough to leave him.

* * *

I took the nightgown from the drawer and held it up to my body. There were wrinkles in the fabric from having been stuffed down into a corner of the drawer. I slipped it over my head and pulled it down over my breasts. The sewn-in cups made me seem fuller than I was. I smoothed the lace and ran my hands over my thighs.

My husband's voice came muted down the hallway. He was tucking Ben in again after a bad dream. I shut the light and got under the covers, then realized I hadn't pulled down the shades. Moonlight came through the windows and lit up the quilt on the bed in places like a dark puddle. I pulled the quilt up to my neck.

He stood in front of the bed and undressed. I watched him go through the ritual stretching and felt a strained desire for the tightly muscled body, but was content only to watch. He slid into bed and snuggled close for the allotted kiss before sleeping. He touched the strap of the red nightie.

"Hello," he said. "What's this?"

I felt my face flush in the dark and shut my eyes. "It's the infamous red nightie," I said, expecting him to laugh, having heard the stories from Dave and old Kevin as they timed each other around the track.

He turned the covers back. "We haven't been properly introduced. How do you do, red nightie?"

I said nothing. I felt his hands begin the slow stroking that preceded our lovemaking. I knew in ten minutes it would be one way, and then ten minutes after that, another. Then it would be over.

His lips found my breast; his fingers began pulling the nightgown away.

"Leave it on," I said, and pulled it back up.

"Are you okay?" he said, and I could see the whites of his

eyes glint in the reflected moonlight, a moment's hesitation before I nodded and he bent back to me.

I pushed the red nightie up to my waist and pressed him against me.

He came. I did too. The nightie bunched up in the small of my back and itched. We parted and went to our respective pillows.

I ran my hands over the hair-thin scar just under the swell of my belly that assured me there would be no more percentages for dominant genes to prevent blood cells from aggregating. It was a given — a kind of heaven in which I could spend myself. My husband went to sleep, his back a pale expanse of flesh and muscle, slowly unknotting, lit by the moon as if cooling down from a great heat.

If I could have asked for music to go with the moonlight, I would have brought the owlet center stage, sent him marching down my husband's back. He would be singing his little heart out: *I love to sing-a, about the moon-a and the June-a and the spring-a. About a sky of blue, a tea for two.*

FIRST CHAIR

We weren't any good and we knew it.

We sat stage left to the conductor, five of us, a two-bit string section composed of ten- to twelve-year-olds. Most of us had had these instruments foisted on us. In my case, it was a genetic fluke that damned me to staring down the hourglass body of the Joseph Bohmann violin — my long fingers — reminiscent of a dead uncle. I took my instruction four afternoons a week, listlessly bowing my arco along with the others, determined to keep my heart out of it. Until First chair started to slip.

Purdy was blond, eleven, his wrists thin as straw. One of those kissy geniuses with a slurry gaze behind thick-lensed glasses. He sat in First chair like it had been invented special just for him. From the row behind, I had a precise view of the back of his head. I became well acquainted with the double-whorl pattern at his crown. During those sleepy practice sessions, I focused on the worn collars of his plaid short-sleeve shirts. A poor kid, his violin borrowed on a Lion's Club scholarship, he had no right to act so proud. His elbows, knots of bone larger than his upper arms, would always lift too high and the conductor would deposit a junior-sized rage upon the entire section, rather than single out his favored student.

What did we think we were, he'd holler, crows flapping around like that?

We were silent in that sea of half and eighth notes, four of us united in a quiet dislike for orchestra, while Purdy, no more talented than any of us, made a ceremony of each note.

Chairs had been assigned early in the school year. The auditions were held in the gym in a choking Indian summer humidity while the smell of old volleyballs mingled with the instructions.

"Read this music," I was prodded by Wadsworth, the conductor, formerly our science teacher.

I shrugged, recited the treble indicated by his pencil. "Every good boy does fine." The bass was a mystery, baited fish hooks under a murky stream I could only guess at. I was assigned Fourth chair. So what? I was only here because my parents had forced me. Fourth wasn't last. There still was Fifth— some nose-picking seventh-grader with a Sears catalogue instrument, painted white to hide the plywood.

* * *

Summer! What kid doesn't mourn it in September, sweating in those hard chairs, alien socks suffocating toughened feet? I daydreamed. My world had gone flat as my temperamental A string. At the Lion's Club carnival in July, Jimmy Laguna and I had each bought chameleons. He was a slow-witted boy from tract houses near the dwindling orange groves, wonderfully disapproved of by my parents. His concave chest was evidence of his mother's prenatal neglect, the harelip scar his own kind of genetic damnation. He wasn't bright, but he could nail a baseball out past second or concoct a firecracker bomb loud enough to make a cat miscarry. Our chameleons were leashed on kite string, the end of which the salesman pinned to our shirts. Jimmy's died that night, but mine was still hanging in there in a screened-over crate out back of my garage. I fed him stunned flies rescued off the sticky paper rolls by my mother's laundry sink. He had no name because he was always changing. I didn't create clever mazes for him, nor beds of fluff. I professed not to love him one way or the other, but he wasn't exactly expendable, like the earthworms we'd dug up after a rain and sent on helium flights. Jimmy tied Dixie cups gondola fashion to the balloon string and we'd sent them journeying.

I'd watched Jimmy's hands set the little red cup free. When it

34

disappeared into the sky, something rattled in me, some neat anxiety I knew I shouldn't be enjoying.

"Going straight to the moon," Jimmy said, as if our worms were part of the space program. "The moon or Mars." Like he believed it.

"Jimmy Laguna," I'd answer. "That stupid worm is only going one place and you know it."

"Where's that?"

"Home to Jesus!"

"No!" Jimmy'd say, his patched-together mouth gone rubbery with fear.

"No, not really," I'd have to tell him. Sometimes twice.

* * *

We started with scales. *See My Pony, Little Pony, I Ride Him All Day.* For tone, for the near-impossibility of keeping time with each other. I resisted the urge to saw Purdy's cowlicks with the tip of my bow. Fifth chair tapped me with an encrusted finger.

"What?" I said. "You better quit touching me unless you can prove you've had a tetanus shot."

He pointed to Purdy. "Listen. First chair's faking. His bow ain't even touching the strings."

"Ever heard of Kleenex?"

I catalogued the information. Purdy wasn't playing. I didn't know if he were bored or lazy, but he was hitting the notes every fifth measure or so.

Even now, school in session, our playtime cut short by having to practice, Jimmy Laguna hadn't abandoned me. He'd call me on the telephone, hook me into arguments saying "Paige, Paige, I got proof my worms made it. Just look outside. Up there on the moon, see that big old shadow? Don't it look about the size of a balloon with the air going out of it?"

Maybe he needed glasses. Try as I might, I couldn't make him understand it was farther away than it seemed.

"The nerve of anyone, calling this late," my mother ranted

and I'd had to lie to assure her it had something to do with orchestra practice.

I studied Purdy and his shining Stradivarius copy. My violin had a permanent stain down the right side of the belly that faded into the f-shaped soundhole. I'd overheard at family gatherings that Uncle tended to drink, playing all those cut-rate birthdays, bar mitzvahs. Maybe it was a spill. It occurred to me that I had been left the violin to make up for that.

Summer still creaked in the grimy transoms, too high even for old Wadsworth to see out. I bet he still thought of science while we hit all those wrong notes. Something to keep him going. I thought of my chameleon, flyless for two days. Today I would catch him some bugs.

The clock ticked on, interminably slow while Purdy went on with his charade. A plan took form in my resentful brain. I couldn't see it clearly just yet, but I could feel it coming. I decided to give Fifth a break. "Hey, you. Quit digging for gold. We're playing on the E string." He gave me a slack-jawed smile.

* * *

"Challenge," Wadsworth explained in a monotone, "is permitted on Thursdays at the end of practice." His sweaty head shone through the long wisps of hair drawn over it. I thought he looked like the illustration of Gregor Mendel in the biology book, all craven and bony like one of his bean crosses. "You may challenge only once during the period. Choose any piece of music we've studied. The more accomplished player wins the higher chair."

Fifth grinned at me. I was calculating, but stared him down like I was bored. In two weeks we would play our first recital, parents invited. Purdy was rosining up his bow, the mother-of-pearl winking from the silver nut. Slacker! I'd give him a week. Then I was going to send him to the moon with Jimmy Laguna's worms and he could fake it for the angels.

36

"Paige has finally found her niche," I heard my mother yakking on the telephone. "Honestly, she practices every waking minute. No more explosions in my flowerbed with that apprentice arsonist from Riverside Drive. It's just lovely. I'm so proud. My daughter, the violinist — the *artiste*."

Nah, Mom. I was a soldier in some children's army, murdering the enemy with my violin. I had a tin ear to the ground, just like Rat Patrol on channel nine. Plans, drills, then the tanks move in for the attack. I wanted to recapture the territory that lay outside my bedroom window. I had chosen the *Danube* because Wadsworth hummed it constantly under his breath, like he could stand our ragged music if he just kept picturing the river. I played with my eyes shut to the carved pineapples atop my four poster. I knew Purdy was dead when I thought of adding the vibrato. Catgut trembled and ached; it could make even a tough guy like Jimmy Laguna cry out uncle.

* * *

One week before our first recital, Wadsworth said hopefully, "Remember, music is not unlike planting a garden. One sows the seeds carefully. Practice, much like watering, must be frequent, even daily. What is to be done now is very important if we expect flowers in the spring. I'm pleased to hear considerable improvement from the wind section." Somebody's tuba farted in protest and he smiled, tolerant. "And I beg of you all — best clothes at the recital. Solid, quiet colors. Pretend it's church, can you?" He let the question settle down on the orchestra, and like fertilizer, we tolerated the stink.

"Now. Are there any challenges?"

I stood up, cradling the Joseph Bohmann, my bow inching upward.

"Well," he said. "Fourth chair?"

I nodded. Purdy sat slumped ahead of me. It never occurred

to the pet he might be called on his string-synching. "Fourth challenges First chair," I said.

Purdy's shoulders shot up unevenly. He turned to face me and his blotchy skin reddened. He was dust, even if I had only asked him to ride the old pony of the scales.

"Piece?" Wadsworth prodded.

"The Danube."

I shut my eyes and summoned a drunken uncle who had to have loved this damn violin enough to pass it on to me. I lifted each note from the stiff horsehair and dragged it mournfully across the stained body. At the vibrato, Wadsworth shook his head in disbelief. I could have quit, it would have been enough. But I saw it through to the last squiggly sixteenth note before I rested.

Purdy rose unsteadily. "I don't have the music."

"Lend you mine," Fifth offered.

I sat in my seat, yanked at a knee sock, fiddled with the turn screw on the bow. Then Purdy played.

The *Danube* wasn't a difficult piece for him. Even rusty, he played all right. Of course, he didn't have the vibrato, but he managed some unnamed spirit I'd had to sweat to conjure. It left me a little haunted.

"Fourth replaces First," Wadsworth announced. The strings were quiet. Purdy picked up his violin and left the room. His chair sat empty.

"Go sit in it," Fifth prodded.

"Don't rush me," I snapped.

"Here's the solo you'll play at the concert," Mr. Wadsworth said, handing me four pages of spidery music.

I held it at arm's length.

"Don't look like that," he told me. "You earned the privilege, now go home and practice."

* * *

Jimmy Laguna set off a cherry bomb on my window sill.

38

Who else but his grubby fingers would place such a gift, like sending me flowers. I studied the splintered wood.

"What was that?" my mother called out from upstairs.

"Car backfiring," I called back.

It was getting cool now, sweaters didn't cut the chill and Jimmy was unmistakable in his patched jacket. "Coming out?" his disembodied lisp begged to me.

My answer was the agonizing solo, over and over from my bed, my chin aching on the ebony rest. If I could have grown small enough to fit in a Dixie cup, I would have opted for Mars.

* * *

I puked before we went on stage, nothing much. Not even Fifth chair, with his bodily obsessions would have found the splash interesting. I straightened my white anklets in the new patent leather Mary-Janes my mother had insisted were necessary for a first recital. I'd kept the business about the solo to myself.

Wadsworth gave me a determined look as we settled ourselves on the raised stage, denying me the luxury of nervousness. He seemed to say this was no different than practice; those people four feet below us were no different than the volleyballs. I dared not turn to look at Purdy in my old seat. When the curtain parted, I could see my mother, everybody smiling at me. Even Jimmy Laguna, scrubbed to an unaccustomed clean, stood in a doorway, near enough to wave at me, not comprehending why I couldn't wave back.

That hour, waiting to play was a lesson I would hold to me for the rest of my life. When parents frighten kids with stories of candy-toting strangers and downed electrical wires, they think screaming is all it takes to drive their fear of your mortality home. But it doesn't, not until you experience the possibility of loss for what it really is. The approaching solo was like staring down a runaway train. I mechanically went though the paces of the music, dead as a metronome inside, my heart ticking. My solo came after the French horns, who mercifully blew the last five notes in double time, thankful comic relief which rustled through the audience like autumn leaves.

I stood, shut my eyes and told my uncle he was a mean old son of a bitch who'd rooked me out of at least an hour's playtime each day for the last five months; what right had he messing with my childhood, I was twelve, for crying out loud. He didn't answer. I played the Mozart with as much dedication as was required, automatic on the rests, precise as the necessary length of strings required on helium balloon gondolas.

Then it was over, Wadsworth shaking my hand, tears in the corners of his eyes — my mother up on the stage shaking with pride. Somehow, I'd pulled it off. While Mother was off with Wadsworth planning my future at Carnegie Hall, Purdy came over.

"You were good, Paige."

"All I did was play. You want to make something of it?"

"That was my solo. I mean to have my chair back."

His smile was smug. His pathetic cowlicks were butch-waxed to his skull. The borrowed violin the color of honey.

"You can have it back, Purdy. I don't give half a duck's green and white crap what you do with it. Me and Fifth just got tired of watching you American Bandstand it. You don't deserve a solo when even a snot eater like that can beat you."

He smoldered under the pronouncement and nearly started to cry. "I been helping my dad in the store and watching my brothers till my Ma gets well. I ran out of time to practice."

I downed a cup of red punch and refused the cake.

"High strung," Mother said to anyone who'd listen. "I'll bet she wants to go home and practice."

Purdy and I looked at each other.

I turned away first. Jimmy Laguna accompanied me. We ran the whole way home through the groves. He knew them as well as cat's cradle; every low branch you had to duck under not to break stride, every stinking smudge pot.

* * *

We planned to set the M-80 into flight, extending the fuse another six inches for a spectacular finale. The damn wind kept blowing it out. I unstrapped my new shoes and went in my stocking feet behind the garage to look for my cache of string. The chameleon's cage was open, just a paper-thin peel of one of his sheddings remained. I checked all the hiding places, remembering that his trick was to blend in. But he was gone.

Jimmy came around the garage and saw me looking. "Jupiter," he told me, a little drool collecting on his scar. "In a real pretty blue cup. He didn't want to go at first, but I taped him down good and no way could he come loose."

The sky was enormous and graying, rain soon, our California version of winter. Old no-name was gone, dead of masking tape and the shock long before the fall. Jimmy grinned at me, gap-tooth stupid.

I knew I could have licked him. He would have chewed grass willingly and swallowed with dignity. He was as my mother had aptly suggested, simple as Chopsticks.

I left him standing there holding the string and went back in my house. The Bohmann lay across my bed right where I'd left it.

My hand curled around the neck lovingly, resting on the wood that was worn soft from my dead uncle's fingers. For the last time, I plucked the four strings that rested over the wooden bridge, that nervy tension some caveman had invented to torture generations.

Then it broke like a peanut shell coming down on the pineapple bedpost. I saw the whole thing in slow motion. The side ribs shattered, the whiskey-colored body splintered into shrapnel. Only the fingerboard stayed all of a piece, still clutched in my hand.

This was the kind of music that would haunt me.

I could hear my mother's good shoes on the wood floor, her quick intake of breath, then her voice. "You are a hateful child, Paige Louise." From farther away, down a generation of hallways, I swore I heard my uncle, *diminuendo*, cheering.

THIRTY-SECOND POSES

I planned it as carefully as a murder. I weighed the alternatives. Whatever happened, there would be no one to blame but myself. Kenneth wouldn't bail me out. He was too busy painting nudes that summer. Besides, he was the reason I was thinking of doing it.

While birds picked at the seed in the raised feeder, I listened to him in the studio off the garage and the idea of an affair came to me. Vague and playful at first, then crystallizing, clear and sharp as if through binoculars. Who hardly mattered. That would be after the fact, much the same as the quick pencil sketches Kenneth made in night class — the thirty-second poses — where the model holds herself in an action pose just long enough for the artist to get the idea of motion down on paper.

It was Kenneth's forte. He could reproduce bodies verbatim from those scribbly lines. They would take form and dimension in the oils he spread on the canvas.

It seemed I'd found the missing link of my constant self-analysis. There between imaginary line of what was absent and what was necessary was the void, a place so sore I could almost put my finger on it. To the left of the line, Kenneth's painting. At first it seemed to me like a foreign language, or maybe this beautiful girl who made me jealous. But no longer. I would have clandestine lunches. I would be special to someone in a secret way. I would learn enough about thirty-second poses to make the nudes move for me in borrowed bedrooms on endless afternoons. I knew just where to go, who to ask.

His reputation preceded his teaching ability. Dr. Hamilton Mead, the very name forcing an on-the-spot evaluation. It was a name that could only be taken seriously, or uttered biting one's lip to keep from laughing. He was the youngest tenured professor in the department and the one I had heard described as a womanizer. I surmised that meant he was the type on which girls developed crushes. That he flirted and dangled his attractiveness like the artifice it was renowned to be. But up until this summer I had no interest in the classes he taught. My studies leaned heavily toward the classics.

Whether or not it was fate that the summer session in Shakespeare was cancelled I will never know. But Contemporary American Mavericks offered me the same number of units. I noted the instructor's name and thought: two birds with one stone. I registered, fully aware that this was the first step, slightly amused that the units earned would help me graduate a semester early.

* * *

"Just think, Annie," Kenneth said, pouring linseed oil on his brushes. "Twelve more units. Then we can work on your PG degree. Which do you want first? Boy or girl?"

What I wanted didn't fit into either category. I shrugged and went into his arms by rote. "Whatever you want," I answered. "Just fill me up. But don't forget to check the oil."

* * *

The first day of class Mead took roll, droning down the attendance sheet as if he were mentally elsewhere. Perhaps out on the bay in a sailboat, or sweating out the last few miles of a rugged stretch of highway between here and Santa Barbara on a mountain bicycle. It could have just been me trying to place us both in that same category of want. The air conditioning was broken. He apologized for it. Sweat gleamed on his forehead trapped in tight curls of hair. He stumbled over my name and his concentration was broken.

44

"An-uh-ees?" he said, giving my first name the workout every uninitiated person did, seeing those side-by-side vowels in print.

I saw the implications in his expression. To him I was just another one of those literature groupies who adopt and discard first names like trendy slang.

"Close enough."

"Any relation to Ms. Nin?" he asked. I supposed he felt it deserved that much.

"An indulgent father," I told him. "He named my brother Sigmund."

That elicited a smile. I gave him my married name. "It would probably be easier to remember if you just called me Johnson."

He shuffled his papers, nodded. A few girls behind me started to titter.

* * *

It was summer. I was ripe for this to happen. At times I thought I'd willed it, spending those hot June nights alone on the Herculon couch waiting for Kenneth to come home from class. The brown and gold idiot weave of the fabric ran together and threatened my plane of vision while I tried to read my textbooks. Lemon-flavored Nestea was my companion, the ice cubes shrugging against each other and dwindling. I had a few worries. The toilet ran constantly in the home we'd bought and the plumber was avoiding my phone calls. Oil paint in quantity might be a carcinogen. My viable eggs were dwindling, sloughed off each month like sand into a timer. I scratched my ankles raw in places, drained my sugary tea and waited for the heat wave to break so I could make my move.

It wasn't just the heat. The summer had buzzed along with purpose. It wasn't like other summers. We had buried my father that May. Though he had been dying by inches for years and it was a relief to see him at rest, his death seemed untimely, as if he still had something to teach me. Yet there was a part of me that

45

seemed to shimmer and vibrate when I pictured myself as parentless, as if I stood alone on a dirt road making my own decision as to direction.

I tried explaining this to Kenneth as he filled in canvas after canvas, the point of his paintbrush fanning out as he lay down the thick, even strokes. I knew he was tired of my words. Just to see if he were listening, I mentioned a 'midnight madness' sale at the local Saylor's. He was off like a shot. For him, that two-for-the-price-of-one kind of thing had more attraction in the thick summer heat than did my circular logic or the state of my ankles.

Classes went well. In my denim skirt and peasant blouse, I felt pristine. I took prolific notes. I wanted to do everything right, aim carefully toward the justified ends. Mead responded. He wrote me messages on the essay exams he handed back.

"Johnson — good point!"

"You have such a fine grasp of this material. Contribute more to class discussions."

Then the payoff: "How come you only wear glasses in the classroom? Are you far-sighted?"

I smiled, took off my glasses when he looked my way. Engineering. It reminded me of that summer when I had wholeheartedly agreed with my father that I was definitely not worth teaching to use a gun. "Absolutely. Female ineptitude," I'd said.

I knew how to get what I wanted. Private lessons plus a new twenty-two of my own.

* * *

The day of the final exam I sat sticky-legged, filling in my blue book. I wrote my concluding paragraph, rose up from my chair and paused only long enough to deposit the essay on his desk. Outside the door, nearly to the stairwell, I was ashamed of myself for plotting so deftly and emerging intact. The sky before me was a dazzling blue, the wind stopped dead. I could hear my own heart beat. The sweat stood above my upper lip and at the muscles in the backs of my knees. I took the tube of cream from

46

my purse and rubbed it into my ankles before they could itch again. Waiting for it to take effect, I breathed deeply, eyes shut. Mead surprised me.

"Coffee," he said, shifting the blue books in a lump under his arm. It wasn't a question. His eyes behind the Ben Franklin glasses caught me holding the uncapped cream. I wondered if this much beauty was an accident, not as practiced as it seemed.

"Coffee?" I echoed. "In this weather?"

"Sure. With crushed ice, maybe a dollop of bourbon. It's been known to cure where other remedies have failed."

He offered coffee. In his spare time, Kenneth painted nudes, none of which were me. What appealed to me most was the idea that I could forsee the progression of events unfold like a kind of second sight.

There was still time to back out, to walk away and have it be nothing more than cute double entendres pencilled in the margins of my essays, but I liked the sound of coffee. It had promise. He was waiting for class to be over. It was a semi-professional code of ethics. I could respect that.

* * *

"See if this doesn't help," he said as he handed me my drink.

"I've always been devoted to tea," I told him. "But I'll give it a try."

"You must come from interesting stock," he said. Little brown coffee beads formed on his moustache.

"Interesting stock? That sounds like cattle. Some hybrid strain especially resistant to hoof rot."

He laughed. "I wouldn't place you there, exactly. I meant the names. Yours — your brother's. What kind of father saddles his children with names so difficult to pronounce?"

"A romantic with strong principles," I offered. "Plus this intense weakness for saddling his children with unpronounceable names."

Mead's smile drew the bar gnats. They seemed to know him,

thought nothing of draping him with a hug. Then the saxophone and guitar players took their places on the small stage and we were deafened. Our conversation was reduced to gestures in the kind of jazz that is supposed to sound more professional the louder it is played.

At my car, Mead took my hand. "Come for lunch tomorrow. I have to do these blue books tonight or I would take you home with me right now."

"You can grade thirty essay tests in one night?"

"Half that," he said. "But then I've got to do the laundry. No clean socks. Or sheets."

* * *

The combination of coffee and bourbon did something to me. I was more than my usual insomniac lying next to Kenneth.

"Make love to me," I begged, hoping it would unwind me, pave the way toward sleep.

"My hands are raw from all that turpentine," he said. "I should quit painting."

"No. Don't quit. You're really good."

"I meant just until my hands heal, Annie. Don't sound so excited."

I bit his neck playfully. "Come on. You don't have to use your hands."

But his thrusts seemed to go right through me and afterwards he fell immediately to sleep. I lay there next to the ghosts in bed like a third party. I could have woken him up and told him where I'd been. He would have forgiven me. Listen, I could say. I've accepted an invitation for lunch and we both know what that means. But I let him sleep.

I had my Nestea. The sturdiness of the couch. I floated in the darkness with no boundaries to moor me.

* * *

48

I drove deliberately slow down the coast highway to Mead's house. Keeping to the right lane I could see the ocean, the kids surfing. I pushed the gear shift knob into neutral and braked to let a group of them cross the highway. Their black wet suits flapped at the ends of their spines like beaver tails.

"Anais," Mead said, pronouncing my name swiftly and easily, opening the door, smiling.

* * *

"More sherry." Mead poured, shifting pillows around himself as he sat facing me on the living room floor.

"Enough," I said, but a beat too late. I was listening to him read aloud from a book of his recently published poems. I hadn't known he wrote poetry. It was hot out. Things were fuzzed all along the edges for me. We had killed over three-quarters of a bottle of Dry Sack.

He stopped mid-poem. "You're uncomfortable. You don't like this room."

I shrugged. "Sure, I do."

"No. I can tell you're evaluating. Be specific. What bothers you?"

I looked around at the things I did like. Upright piano painted an awful pea green. The cerulean tilework on the hearth. "It's the shag carpeting," I told him. "It doesn't belong. What's underneath?"

"Oak planking. This used to be my grandfather's place. When he rented it out, the tenants complained wood floors were passe."

"That's insane. How can wood ever be out of style?"

He tipped his glass and finished his drink, went to the kitchen and came back with a couple of paring knives. "Begin anywhere you like," he told me.

I did, falling in love with the idea that we two made some kind of picture down on our hands and knees, pulling up staples and furring strips, getting dusty and sweaty.

49

"Not bad time," I said when we were finished.

"About as long as it takes me to grade essays."

"You're exaggerating."

"I never exaggerate." He moved closer. I could see the blue of his eyes, rimmed in the wire glasses. They shone as if to say: this is as far as I go. I bare my scarred floor and give you a knife, but where we go from here is up to you.

I started to reach up to him, invoking a shiver in the heated silence. My dusty hand went maybe three inches before he was on me. Kissing, stroking my hair, murmuring small words as if he had just been waiting. I dropped the knife and it clattered on the floor.

"Cut up a little carpet and you turn into an animal," I said.

"I'll have to remember that."

He laughed. "You started it. Remember *that*."

I let him carry me into his bedroom and undress me, though I was too aware to feel much sexually. I felt myself move in tune with his rhythms, rock to the cadence of his body, drift off into a corner somewhere while he spent himself.

* * *

The dust fell softly from the cornstarch spreading in clouds over the water in the toilet as I powdered my diaphragm, checking the rim for cracks. Before Mead, before Kenneth. It was a demanding ritual. With Kenneth, I would wait until he was quiet, reach my hands out to find him in the dark, searching. Taking, I felt from his hands, the essence of the nudes, the pigments that made the flesh tones come to life. It would relax him, but wind me up tighter until the pressure was more than I could bear. Then I would disentangle from the sheets and go downstairs for another eight-hour shift on the couch, staring until my eyes felt like empty black sockets. I travelled back twenty years, looking for something.

My father'd taught me to shoot with an old-twelve gauge. How to position the gun butt up against my shoulder. He spoke calmly to assure me. Said to draw in a breath, let it out as I squeezed the trigger, slowly, gently.

"What about recoil?" I said. My brother had warned me. "Don't borrow trouble," Father had answered. "Stop antici-pating. Follow directions. Let it be a total fluid motion. Your shoulder won't even realize what's happening."

"Daddy?" I ran my fingers along the engraved stock, the raised wood of my new .22. "Can you kill a person with a gun this size?"

"Why? You thinking of offing Sigmund? It takes three things. A projectile," he said, and held up the slim bullet in his stocky fingers. "A gun." He lay the rifle across his thighs and loaded the shell. Then he pinched my nose. "One more thing. An idiot stupid enough to aim at something other than the intended target."

* * *

I lay in Mead's bed, dozing. It was eleven, maybe twelve o'clock. I was full from the dinner, the wine, the sex. He slept next to me, his beard curling in the crook of my arm. He breath was noisy against my breast.

Sometime later I woke alone, startled, remembering my clever lie, that Kenneth didn't expect me home. I took a deep breath to relax. Mead stood in the doorway. I caught the glint from his glasses in the darkness. He held a bottle of wine by the neck and a bowl of grapes he'd just picked from the arbor out back where the shag carpeting lay rolled, awaiting a trip to the dump. The grapes were hot and sweet as he popped them into my mouth, first with his fingers, then with his tongue.

It started to rain.

* * *

"Fall semester is one week away," he told me one afternoon

51

as I dangled my feet over the edge of his sailboat, dipping them in the water so it made the image I had no feet at all.

"Right. I still need to pay my tuition."

"We need to talk."

"About what?" I knew what. Lazy and brown, I wanted to soak up the last bit of summer. Winter meant sheeting rain and half the trees still grinning at you green.

"How we proceed. You and I. Discretion."

"I understand the ground rules. You don't need to explain."

I could tell he wanted to say more. The boat needed a lot of maintenance. He was devoted to it. I watched the back of his neck as he dipped a paintbrush into varnish the color of honey.

"Remember when we ripped up your rug?"

"Yeah. I was half-crazy wanting you. That rug will cost a couple hundred dollars to replace."

"You have to admit the room looks a lot better."

He turned to face me. "You were right. I'm adult enough to admit it. And cheap enough to wish I'd brought the rug back into the garage before it rained."

"Why?"

"I'm thinking of renting the place out, try living on the boat for a semester."

"Then what?"

"My sabbatical. Maybe you'd like to try sailing to Hawaii."

I pressed my fingertips into the freshly painted decking.

"Anais, cut that out." He frowned and pulled my hand away.

"They won't stay," I explained. "Varnish moves a little when it dries. The marks won't even show."

"How do you know?"

"I'm married. To an artist."

He set the brush on the lip of the can and studied it. "Is that all? I thought maybe you were trying to tell me to stop this and pay a little more attention to you."

"That, too."

He gave me a hug that I returned a beat too late. Our rhythm was gone.

"Just don't put the rug back," I whispered before I broke away. "Keep the floor bare."

His face was open to me then. With one gesture, I could have changed the entire landscape. Shot the moon. But I didn't.

If anything, I was the twelve-year-old Anais whose pigtails lay flat and orderly against her back, her neck freckled from the sun as she lay quiet, horizontal in the grass, hearing her father's whispers about what kind of a bird it might be, the butt of the gun backed into proper position. The twelve-year-old woman who could shoot, gut the bird and still revere life as she brought down only the intended target, saving the top knot feathers from a mountain quail, stuffing them into her flannel shirt pocket as a kind of trophy. I had just forgotten.

* * *

It had been a summer like that, with hums from the refrigerator I had neglected to defrost. With the ice cube trays sliding in and out easily from a little cave in the front because I needed them to make the daily Nestea. With Mama Lucci's famous easy-to-fix spaghetti dinners that came in the three-compartmented plastic trays I used and reused, even though the grease would not come off entirely and occasionally I would foul a dishcloth with the orange film that could have waxed a million tables and still remained practical, useable. It was a summer, longer than others. Kenneth sold his first painting and framed a dollar bill. I dug through closets until I found a shotgun shell that I kept in my purse and would reach in at various times to grip in my palm — for distance, for measure, for how much I had grown since twelve.

BABY STEPS

Chelsea and I, sitting on my bed one night in the apartment above the surfboard wax factory, were (when weren't we?) commiserating — offering and rejecting a gazillion theories on why I should file a formal complaint against the professor who made a pass at me.

"He's a pig," she'd offered. "It's up to you to stop him dead in his rut. Turn him in. Something like a nice sexual harrasment suit. Make him sweat before he loses his job."

"I don't want that. I just want him to say he's sorry. That's all."

"Pocket change," she said. "Go for the entire purse."

Her thin tanned arm waved my words off, making a poetic arch against the pillow ticking, the blond pine paneling that cried out for posters, poor reproductions of Chagall, anything but the sad watermarked past.

And she had sound reasoning on her side, I knew.

But I'd vacillated too long. Even Chelsea would admit we were beating a dead horse.

At first she was like the other girls I'd known, in a sweet jealous awe over my basketball prowess, thinking if she touched me, it would rub off. At times it was like being sisters, wanting that momentary closeness to be with you for life, then rankled to the point of murder when she'd take my one and only Calvin blazer and leave it in some guy's Volkswagen Rabbit, or inconsiderately use the last mini-pad. Chelsea was all those things as well as too beautiful for her own good. It's an old story, and I know it sounds like I'm whining, but truly I'm not ugly, even if I cannot forget the rutting pig's words one afternoon when I waltzed into his class-room in a new dress.

I was late; a quality he despised. Before I could sit, he some-how connected a polar tension between chronic lateness and my crepe dress: "You can put the ugliest girl in the world into a beau-tiful dress, and what do you have, class?" As usual, no one answered so he filled in his own blanks. "At best, just a beautiful dress."

Chelsea'd taught me how to outline my lips in mauve pencil so they looked cultured and thin, but promising; she always cheered me up. But she was not in the Literature building when I reentered, repeating to myself, you are matriculating here, this is the act of a responsible adult who does not hold grudges past three semesters. Eyes up, shoulders back, let's make those breasts cry out Dolly! You'll kick ass in English Composition. This professor's an easy A. He'll exclaim (inwardly of course), my God, finally, someone who knows how to use grammar. He'll sit gratefully down on the table at the front of the room and it too will creak happily; she's back, let those individual gems of prosody land on me, please, I've almost got enough to make a necklace.

The rutting pig would not be delighted to hear I was trotting his halls. But we would not fraternize in any case. A book from the library I now owed half a month's rent on had the whole thing in a nutshell:

> Consistent with all cultures is punishment. Severe dis-approval results in castigation; forms vary. It is in this author's opinion that cruelest of all is the practice of the Huniga Indians, who affect the silent treatment when a member of the tribe has fallen out of favor.

There was more. I'd studied it. Fantasized many times how the pig and I might bump elbows, if a little fuzzy on what would follow.

Could "Forgive me?" tremble on such an agile moustache? Did I want him to beg?

Nothing too humiliating. Just slow his pace so that for once his thumbs dangled empty, and somebody's nipples stayed safely enclosed in bra, under camisole, shirt buttoned to the neck.

No answers in that book. Or down this hallway, this thirty-mile hike for which I would earn no particular badge.

I considered drawing eyepatches on his faculty picture, changing the lettering on his lecture announcements to filthy words. But I'm chicken, the furthest I got was his help-wanted ad on the bulletin board:

Wanted: student as part-time secretary. Must have own transportation. Must have typing skills. Must be able to read illegible writing.
Must have current tetanus vaccine.

My Palmer method handwriting added. My recognizable lavender ink pen, a gift from the pig in earlier days, when we frequented the same trough.

Okay, so there's an element of exaggeration here. I tend to embroider what too starkly viewed gives me a tummy ache. I will come clean. It was not a surfboard wax factory. I didn't sit in bed, sniffing musk on Mondays, frangipani on Thursdays. I wasn't always watching *Simon and Simon* and falling in love with brother Rick's outback cowboy hat's pinch-front crease. But that hat did touch me. Show me a girl who denies that deep down she doesn't love a cowboy. There's your liar. And if it wasn't me alone in that apartment on the corner of Main and Pacific Coast Highway, so what? I drove past it so many times I imagined it could have been. So maybe it seems like an enormous fabrication — this laddered story where the bullshit piles up in each rung your foot exits. But I'm taking steps toward the truth. Even if they are baby steps.

I have never done it for money. I have always approached the pebbly surface of that brick-orange basketball out of love and respect. How can it be anything but spiritual? You've got the whole world in your hands. Consider the grace of the opposing thumb sending the sphere forcefully toward the hoop, the string net gratefully opening up to receive and release. I say get rid of the Lakers, who tease everyone into believing they can do it, then hand the game over to some lame team like the Golden State Warriors in the last ten minutes. Clearly, this is a woman's sport, all that's needed for success is aligning the team's menstrual cycles. Take care of the details and it's as simple as symbolic ovulation, regulation swollen egg, Fallopian hoop, send them down regular, hook shots, free throws, those one-in-a-million court-long swoops, we can do them all every twenty-eight days.

Some of us can. It comes natural.

Not Chelsea. Six years of Vermont boarding schools under her Norma Kamali belt and still she wanted to be me — this hybrid California girl who grew up playing HORSE in driveway courts, using bent coat hangers to form the hoop. The me I'd worked to perfect. She wanted to step into my high-tops and own all those choice shots. I understand — I don't much like it — but I comprehend it. Now. Then I was caught up signing life-sized posters she had printed of me. "I look at your calf muscles," she'd told me, tears in her eyes. "I'm sitting on the john looking and I know I can lift weights and run myself to the bone and I'll never have your calf muscles."

"Eat," I told her. "Pasta, cashews, whole loaves of bread. That's your problem. You survive on a Cobb salad once a week down at Uncle Dougie's diner and you wonder why you can't develop extensors and flexors." I did everything but hand her the fork. I showed her my shortcuts. That to make up for my petite stature I made considerable use of the feint. Where to tape her ankles to minimize the stress to an already weak joint.

She relied on her yellow satin tank top and glittering shoelaces to get her on the team. She was a lot like a sister. She never let me get away with sighs and secret moping.

"I don't really have secrets," I told her. "I tell you everything. He was an old friend that I trusted who hurt me."

"Be serious. He's a pig. Pigs rut."

I guess a pig ruts. Not in the sexual sense of the word. More out of habit, because no one teaches him otherwise. So he wasn't really a pig, he was a Rut. The trouble with ruts is manifold. One trips continually, never learning that a rut is a rut is a rut, which may sound like some Dr. Seuss version of theosophy, but is as concrete as torn metatarsal arches and the stink of Absorbine, Jr. He rutted back when we were just out of our teens, anxious in our first year of college, a couple of terriers trying out pissing with the big dogs. Acceptance into different packs separated us. Then we parted.

And re-met when I enrolled in his workshop: Life Scripts. The drama of dreams. The metaphysical horseshit of the unconscious that we as students would technically attach to paper. What did we hope for? Brilliance? A fast-food psychoanalysis? Maybe just to be shown that our grainy lives could finally come alive set on a stage, all lit up.

We were hard to reach. He had us arrange our chairs in a circle, a horseshoe, a triangle. Collective ass flesh going to pins and needles in those molded buckets, no place to rest your feet. We were timid, our dialogues were clutched to the chest, tiny print in notebooks as varied as colors in the spectrum.

But the rut widens to include a few select voices each semester and I walked that road myself. Oh, I'd like to say I slipped, fell there, sprained something vital and had to sit awhile and mend, but that's more of an exaggeration than me as a basketball star. Do you see a pattern emerging here? Sometimes for attention one leads with libido. It was spring. Attach your own impetus. Lonely, I went.

Let me explain about basketball. I'm as short as the lyrics in the Randy Newman song. I wish fiercely I'd make somebody's team. Just the idea of a team. But I'm not Shirley MacLaine, I'm tethered to a dirt court and don't much believe people can or should direct one another, much less cheer toward a common goal. I watch ESPN and want to cheer on the Lakers, *my boys*, Jack Nicholson calls them, but I know ultimately they're human, bound for some failures. It's not me specifically they're letting down, it's the build-up of lactic acid or the ADP factor in muscle, just some tall boys getting plain old tuckered out. So don't fault me for lying. Didn't Michelangelo use ladders? Have some kind of teacher?

Students sign up for courses grudgingly, they all do. They want something that doesn't meet too early, doesn't interfere with lunch, ends early enough that they can still go surfing and is transferable. Teachers want the same thing. The only difference is they get paid for it. A student with talent is gravy, one in a miniskirt wearing new white cotton underpants buttercream frosting on a bran muffin vocation.

I learned this from him: From inside the rut, one does not include the word no as a viable answer. He didn't. Not since his mother had slapped his hand out of the Waterford candy dish in the living room and discovered the idea of matinees as the perfect babysitter. She had time to play cards with the ladies and he was schooled too well — all life is scripts — be it Comedy, where you're both spitting Cherry Coke and holding your sides, Drama, where you take the time to listen with the furrowed brow you've paper clipped as the correct concerned expression, or Tragedy, where sometimes old friends get wounded in an inaccessible place that produces only scar tissue.

He loved best his movie posters from *Variety*. Those 15 x 24 glossy card stock color fold-outs the magazine offers up at Academy Award time. I think afternoons of Westerns warped him into believing the way to behave toward a woman is to yee-hah-gallop up spraying dirt and slap her around a few times. Good-natured, I-want-in-your-prairie-skirt-spanking. Just enough to get the blood flowing. Pinken the skin. Don't bother to water the horse or check his shoes, just tie his reins to the nearest hitching post and head on upstairs hand in hand. Tomorrow, do it again, but never with the same actress, maybe a red-haired woman this time, just to see if what they say is true about redheads down there.

He had this poster in ML-135, this *Variety* freebie of Sam Shepard and Kim (take me to your icebox) Basinger. I'd stared at it over too many semesters, trying to figure it out. Was the game to guess which one was the bigger fool for love? He had it tacked up real high, stapled six times, those institutional staples. It was in an exalted location, above the chalkboard, to the left of his podium. The rest of the room was checkerboarded with old movie posters, Pauline Kael reviews, throwaway stuff, penny-ante.

Re-entering that room, my last semester, it was the first thing I saw. A dare thrown out to me, some pale giant on the away team, calling me dyke. From where I sat facing a new professor, one more interested in my prose than my chest profile, I need not have focused so high. But I was looking for a horizon of sorts. Where I was headed next. I wasn't asking map, just direction.

I suppose I could have thrown the I Ching, fed my bio-rhythms to the Microsoft Basic disk on my Kaypro 2X. Rented a dark car. Slunk cat-hammed into an unlit room. But all I had to do was chat with the janitor for a few minutes. Listening to somebody's life story works better than a bribe.

Then I committed my singular criminal act of thirty-odd years lifetime, and it was a bigger letdown than watching Kareem fumble the ball by the hoop into Larry's waiting hands, than the time Chelsea pulled up her shirt and showed me her auxiliary tits, some defective gene in her chlorinated chromosome pool that Bennington and old money couldn't quite cover, than discovering I did indeed have a G-spot and now what.

Of course, gaining what I'd come for, I lost something. My purse spilled on the tabletop as I dragged it to the chalkboard. I worked up quite a sweat using my nail file on those staples. Somewhere in the rush of adrenalin I lost my lavender pen, like offering my own petty evidence. But I commandeered the poster. Sam Shepard was mine. Kim dwindled in significance, but on side two, the side that had been turned to the wall, she dominated, bigger and stronger than Sam's horse, some 17-hand bulldog quarter all gimmicked up with martingales and trick bits. It seemed like a message.

Chelsea left me for this amazing girl who could work miracles at the free-throw line. I became a vague memory, for the moment at an impasse, like how it feels waiting for GRE scores. She took her platinum smile and proffered friendship and kept a few of my things I wanted back, not so much for the monetary as the intrinsic sentiment. My old sweat band, a roll of duct tape, the secret jump shot she was now claiming as hers all along. And I was not surprised. Just as I expected the pig to continue to rut, and the halls here to grow too narrow to hold me, all those things happened.

But what I didn't expect was how it felt growing out of it — that in passing the ball permanently there would be such an unburdening, a distaff freedom. I couldn't resent Chelsea for going after what she wanted. And I couldn't hate the Rut any more, but I also could no longer love him. I needed six inches of sorry and he just could not get it up. There would never be an apology because my truths and his were as diverse as surfboard wax and cowboy hats. It was time to stop fabricating cushions for that old bone — betrayal.

But I had something. Custody of the poster, the representation of all of our life scripts, the whole sad incestuous story. I took it home. Framed it. Lovingly, like a hard-earned diploma.

It is out of deference to truth that I put pen to paper and scratch this rough script:

Just before CURTAIN FALLS:

(*exit CHELSEA, holding basketball shoes, out stage-left door, defects like kitten teats, sweet and hidden. Exit, RUT, stage right door, chewing loudly, the audience is given to understand the trial and failure to teach table manners. Only THE THIEF remains.*

Alone, center stage, arms spread toward the audience as if expecting judgment, hoping forgiveness. She turns, looking over her shoulder as if into an imaginary desert sunset where the gaudy colors cannot be misinterpreted. It is clear no one's won here; they are just a couple more fools for love, repeating old mistakes. Now the lights fade to black. I'm sure you get the picture. So why don't you pick the music.)

HANK AND CHLOE:
Love and Death Ride the Same Pony

GEOGRAPHICS

While Hank's folks were in Europe on one of those budget tours for seniors — twenty-two stops in twenty-eight days — Uncle Bob started dying. Seriously, this time. He was over eighty and had been in a rest home for years.

Hank wasn't positive whether Uncle Bob was his great uncle on his father's side or his mother's. Only when his folks spoke of coordinating their errands around checking on Uncle Bob, was he reminded the old man existed at all.

"You might say we kill two birds with one stone," Hank's father would say.

"At the very least manage to wound them," Chloe, Hank's girlfriend would mutter.

Hank, enduring their monthly visits, did not say much of anything. The way he saw it, there was a fine line down the middle of both relationships, parents versus girlfriend, and a meditative posture was necessary to maintain balance.

However, while they were gone, the nursing home began to call him. As next of kin, he could sense in the nurse's voice that someone should be making plans on behalf of the family. It was the first time in thirty-five years he could recall regretting being an only child.

"Is a hospice really necessary?" he asked the nurse.

"It was your uncle's idea."

Hank felt backed into a corner of his office, the same way he did when a student would come in to complain missing an A grade by a few points. Sometimes he just gave them the higher mark, departmental procedures be damned, glad when they left him alone.

"If you want to visit," the nurse said, "now would be a good time."

"I'll be by tomorrow. Around noon." He hung up the phone, the black receiver in his palm so slippery with sweat it might have been an eel.

* * *

The European itinerary his parents had left was incomplete. His father had marked their hotel names and dates in two colors of marker pen, but after the twenty-ninth, the schedule read Ireland.

"Not Dublin, not Killarney, not even 'we'll pick up some great bargains at the Waterford factory,' just Ireland."

"Maybe one of his pens ran out," Chloe suggested. "This is probably the first time in his life he's left anything open-ended. You should be congratulating him. It's a whole new direction."

Standing in the kitchen, licking a knife that dripped peanut butter, she looked ten years old, not twenty-nine. "Listen," he told her, "spontaneity I could applaud, but short of flying over there and traipsing the old sod, how am I supposed to touch base with them? You think there's an Irish equivalent of the Canadian mounties? What do I tell them? 'Be on the lookout for two old people armed with lists and tight schedules?'"

She set the knife down and licked her fingers. "Do you have any idea how hot it makes me when you get all overwrought like this? Jesus, come here."

There was a certain numbness that descended when the phone would ring the third Thursday night of each month. Chloe'd be curled up on the couch cleaning tack and without looking up she'd say: "It's them, you get it." And if he didn't,

64

she'd let the phone ring itself out. Hank would feel his chest constrict, as if somewhere inside things were bracing themselves. He imagined his organs girding, preparing for a drift that would leave untenable gaps.

Chloe had a point. His parents seemed determined to keep him anchored in the past. They sent him letters full of clippings from the *Times* — articles on premature hair loss tied to a diet high in junk food, sad missives on the impending extinction of the California condor, curiosities like a story in which a 1965 Rambler American (the same model and year car he'd first learned to drive) falling into a Florida sinkhole. He wasn't sure if these examples were intended to be metaphoric of his life or earthly imbalances they expected him to correct.

Once on what Hank assumed to be a purely nostalgic note, his mother had included a 'milk money' bank book he'd kept in the fourth grade. He supposed the bottom line was righteous mother indignation pointing out that the Valley National Bank was in possession of Henry Oliver's nickels, that he was entitled to ask for them back plus interest. He smiled at his wobbly cursive; the O in Oliver sagged left of center. The hell with the money, what he liked was the sturdy fabric cover of the book and the dual wheels one wound string around to close the envelope. He pushed a thumbtack through the card onto Chloe's bulletin board, next to the calendar of Secretariat, retired and grazing, nothing to do but service the mares.

Chloe, who never touched his mail except to lay it on the table and smirk if their return address was among the envelopes, delivered her usual remarks.

"Next I expect they'll send you all your baby teeth, strung together like a set of matched pearls. Don't they ever throw anything away?"

He had taken her in his arms and flashed a mournful smile. "You mean that business about the tooth fairy planting baby teeth in the sky to grow new stars was a lie?"

He would see his uncle because it had to be done. Chloe

could say what she wanted, but the truth was, at times she was just as backward as his parents.

For instance, she didn't believe their marrying necessary until something of value was involved. "Like real estate," she'd told him. "Say if we bought a house." Hank had circled possibilites in the newspaper, but Chloe rejected them all for the same reason. There was no place to keep her horse, Absalom. It was a pretentious name, Methuselah would have been more appropriate. He was a twenty-one-year-old gelding that had more than earned his right to be put out to pasture, yet Chloe insisted he still had a few good rides in him. It sounded to Hank like she was discussing the amount of tread left on the Michelins.

Yet what she gave, she gave willingly. A bite of marmalade toast while he was watching a special on PBS. He liked the taste of her neck, all salt, after she exercised the horse. They were down-to-earth offerings from a girl who would never be considered more than attractive. It wasn't just her coarse mouth that set wrong with his folks. Both his parents had expressed wanting for Hank someone exotic, foreign. Chloe would be none of those things, even if he took her to Europe. She was all too aware of their desires and how short she fell. Once, playing *Trivial Pursuit* with his folks, she'd argued his father to the mat, stating flatly that Africa *was too* a country. Hank shushed her, pointing out in the encyclopedia that it was a continent, a land mass all its own. She seemed genuinely befuddled, then confessed she'd only been two places in her life, California and Texas.

"I can't imagine what lies beyond," she'd said.

"That's all right. They're good places to know. For the most part, Africa can't hold a candle to them."

"You're just saying that to make me feel less stupid."

"What about Sam Shepard? To listen to him, you'd think the two most important places in the world are California and Texas."

"Ha. You put anyone into space and they get a different perspective. What's that got to do with Africa?"

It took him a minute to make the connection, her thinking

astronaut, not playwright. "Okay, maybe nothing. But you two would get along. He has this thing about horses."

She gave him a look, still slightly smoldering, but wanting reassurance.

There was nothing so naive about the country of their living room during his parents' visits. Chloe would perch resentfully in the rocking chair, her cowboy boots drawn up, her very posture an accusation. His parents would take the couch, facing Hank as if his girlfriend were a border town they wanted to pretend did not exist.

For his father's birthday, she'd baked gingerbread and stood in the living room singing "Happy birthday to you," unabashed at her lonesome tenor. It didn't matter to her that they rarely celebrated beyond exchanging cards, hadn't sung out loud since Hank was a kid.

Then his mother, looking at Chloe's boots had asked: "Don't you find that large animals require quite a bit of cleaning? Not to mention the element of disease."

"They have the same functions as we do," Chloe'd said, slicing the cake. "They shit and get sick, if that's what you mean."

"But it must make you so *tired*, dear. You can't possibly get enough rest."

"A cup of Earl Grey to go along with this lovely gingerbread," Hank had offered, and the moment had been stifled.

"Take a rest my sweet ass," Chloe had hissed as they drove away. "What does she think I am? Weak with the vapors because I can muck out a stall or puny because you keep me up fucking all night?"

* * *

"He will be very emotional," the nurse said as they spoke outside Uncle Bob's room. "It's important for him to talk. Just listen, go along with his train of thought, no matter how disconnected it may seem."

Chloe squeezed Hank's hand. "How long should we stay?"

"As long as he seems to want you. I'll check back in ten minutes."

"Great," Hank said as she walked away. "She'll get involved with bedpans and forget us."

"Try entertaining the idea of relaxing. That poor old man's going to take one look at you and offer you the bed."

Hank stopped. "Look, I can't go in there just yet. I need to walk around, get a cup of coffee or something."

"Right now?" He didn't answer, but wound his way through corridors, breathing shallowly when the scent of alcohol or hot food threatened to choke him. He halted in the cafeteria, poured himself a cup of coffee and sat down at one of the formica tables. He flipped through a magazine with a photo of a gorilla cuddling a baby kitten.

Even away, they weren't gone. The photographs they left, somehow foreign and accusing, the old clothes bought at a neighbor's garage sale, the worst being the *National Geographics* they would lug out of the trunk.

"You're artistic," his mother would say. "You could cut up the pictures and make a collage."

"Some interesting facts in here," his father would say, thumping a cover with a Balinese woman balancing a pottery bowl on her head.

"Please," Hank would say, then falter as the weight of just a dozen or so seemed not entirely unmanageable. His garage was thick with them. It wasn't unsightly, it was a fire hazard. They slid into each other, planting themselves, growing.

His coffee was cold. Chloe was probably pacing the hallway, ready to hand him his backside though she would make it a point to say ass.

He asked for her at the nurse's desk and was told she'd gone inside. He pushed open the door, prepared for the worst.

It was a hospice; it was supposed to be comforting that Uncle Bob lay in a four-poster, the covers household faded, the flowery print scattered over the pillowslip like constellations. It made him look not as bad as expected, yellowish, a little shrunken. But the tube that disappeared into his arm was unmistakably businesslike.

Chloe, boots resting on the bedrail, said "Finally. A witness for the defense. Ask him yourself, Bob."

"Ask me what?"

"Uncle Bob doesn't believe me about the rodeo circuit. I told him about the ribbons for barrel racing and showed him the scar on my leg where the horse bit me, but it's no go. You tell him. Your girlfriend's no lady, just a horse bum."

Absalom did bite her, but the rest is a lie. She rides in an English saddle and looks down her nose at Western paraphernalia.

"Sure," he told the old man. "They're faded, but the living room wall sports a few blue ribbons."

Chloe bent to give the old man a kiss. "I'm going to the ladies. You two spend some time together."

"So," Hank says, then realizes this is stupid way to begin a conversation with a dying man.

"Sow what you reap," Uncle Bob answers. "That sounds like your father and his old sayings. He always has a quote to give me."

"I'm sorry they're not back from Europe."

"Just between you and me, I'd sooner take a visit from that young lady of yours. What style! That business about the rodeo's malarkey, isn't it?"

"The horse is quite real. Sometimes I think she loves him more than she does me."

Hank is surprised at himself for saying this. Chloe doesn't really throw Absalom in his face. The horse exists, as much a part of his life as the maps that spill out of the *Geographics*, unread.

Uncle Bob cleared his throat, an event that took ten minutes. "So. Tell me how the Lakers are doing. I try to listen to the TV, but I can't make out what they're saying. Ears are going."

"They gave it away to the Celtics. It was pretty much to be expected, part of their pattern."

Uncle Bob's grip on Hank's hand is surprisingly strong. "It all comes down to patterns, doesn't it, son?"

"This move to the hospice — are you sure? We could arrange to switch you back."

"They way I see it, one place is as much the same as another." He compressed his lips. "Now that's malarkey. It was the hardest decision I had to make. But it's where I belong."

His breath comes in little sucks, as if he can't get his lips wet enough. Hank is reminded of students who come to his classes stoned.

"Listen," Uncle Bob says. "I just want to tell you this one thing. I can't seem to let it rest until I do. You should be together more, just get together. Will you do that? Promise?"

"Of course." He has no idea what his uncle means together — but the nurse said to agree and he does.

As if his thought is her cue, she enters the room. "Time for your medication."

Uncle Bob turns his head, looking expectant.

Hank shook his uncle's hand because he wasn't sure about kissing him. He feels that something is missing, something he was supposed to say or some connection they were supposed to make hasn't happened. He stands there for a moment. "Chloe's horse is backward," he tells his uncle. "He thinks the idea is to knock down as many barrels as you can." He lets the hand go. "Be seeing you."

Uncle Bob's eyes after his medication are seemingly all pupils, glittering birdlike in the skull. "I expect you will. Kiss the girl for me?"

He does. So often Chloe makes him pull over and let her drive home.

"Blurt it out, Hank. You hold too much inside."

He can't, but she's right. Horse manure tracked on the living room floor can be swept away, as well as her ignorance of geography, but he could almost leave her for her ability to see through his defenses.

She is more than a little like Absalom; both seem outside the

70

brotherhood of the species. Hank has stood at the pipe fence and watched Chloe move the old gelding through his paces. On a good day, with subtle leg pressure, she coaxes him over the three-foot fences evoking an athlete's grace that puts one in mind of his past, a blue ribbon clipped to that chrome ring connecting bit to rein.

He makes up his mind he will find them a house, even if he has to build a loft above the damn hay shoot. They'll move out of that apartment, and they'll do it together.

* * *

Uncle Bob has been buried for twelve days when he tracks his folks down through the travel agent. He had the airline radio ahead that they should meet him outside customs where he will break the news and drive them home.

He wondered how it was for them, circling the airport in a traffic pattern, with the message that he is there to meet them. They will undoubtedly conclude Uncle Bob's death. Otherwise he would never take a day off work to drive them home. He has been more than adept at keeping the relationship brief. Perhaps they should get together more often, as Uncle Bob suggested, but Hank doesn't see how the four of them around a table in Denny's will change what is an organized and balanced pattern of behavior.

Now he can see their heads above the long line at customs. His father's sporting an Irish hat that seems too small. His mother is jaunty in mock Royal Stewart trousers. They wave to him. Finally they are released into the waiting area and come toward Hank with resignation on their faces.

"Uncle Bob passed, didn't he?" his mother said.

"It's okay you weren't here," he quickly put in. "We managed all right."

But it isn't okay. Nobody's done anything heroic unless it's Uncle Bob, knowing when to make the call to the hospice. Hank's suddenly angry at everything: his father's silly hat, the

T-shirt his mother brought from Cambridge, Chloe, trying to be nice, pretending to admire it.

He imagines leaving them all here, making some excuse about needing to visit the men's, then putting pedal to the metal all the way out to the stables. He's watched Chloe do it enough times he could manage to get the halter on the horse. The worst that could happen is he might bite, but Hank doesn't bruise that easily.

He wondered what would happen if he did this, unhooking the halter and just walking away, leaving the horse free of restraint for once in his life. Would he run? Full gallop up the grassy hills behind the stable, charging at the grasshopper oil pumps sucking the land an inch lower each year? Or would he just stand there, patiently waiting for some kind of instruction, direction?

"Africa," he'd tell him. "Now there's the place you want to go. It's this giant land mass where you can get it together. Your pick of pasture. You don't even need an itinerary."

"You know," Hank's father is saying, "when we go through Uncle Bob's things we'll put some aside for you. You'd like that, wouldn't you, son?"

Hank pats his shoulder, taking the carry-on luggage from him. He could explain about the last day with Uncle Bob, how he talked a blue streak, then just as suddenly choked for breath and was silent. How that silence in itself is his gift, something Hank will hold to himself forever. But he knows his father won't hear. He's in a snit now, fighting with his mother over the baggage claim checks. If it isn't too late, Hank would like nothing better than to send them back to Ireland.

He feels Chloe staring at him from across the other side of the baggage carousel. It is as if they are the only two people in the terminal.

She takes her index fingers and taps them against her front teeth. "Baby stars?" she whispers, the softness in her voice surprising.

"Malarkey," he answers, seriously, for Uncle Bob.

72

FIGURES FROM A FUNERAL PROCESSION

The way Hank is sighing reminds Chloe how her foster father, Ben Gilpin, used to make a similiar noise when events went belly-up: his day, the transmission on the Ford pickup, Chloe's first attempt at a permanent wave. The sound was hopeless, but sincere, measured in equal portions for wrecked hair or mainshaft bearings. "Always tell the truth," he'd said to her, the summation of seven years of fatherly advice. "I'm not saying it will set you free, but in the end, folks will respect you for it."

Nested in tissue paper in Chloe's lap are three carved Chinese figurines, members of a funeral procession. The wooden faces are antique, peaceful, flawless. The eyes follow her everywhere. Next to Chloe sits Hank, the man she lives with. Seated across from the two of them, his smiling parents, both in their seventies, wait to hear what Chloe thinks of her present.

Iris, Hank's mother, has spent the last six months battling cancer. She has kept her beautiful silver hair, despite the rigors of therapy. Earlier, in the kitchen, she confided to Chloe that Hank's father, Charles, will no longer sleep with her. Try as she might, Chloe can't get the idea out of her head. Chloe looks at Charles and thinks: pea green sofa bed. She has slept there once herself and there is a spring that stabs you, no matter how you contort your body.

"These look as if they belong in a museum," she finally says.

"Nope, nope. Museum didn't want them," Charles answers. "I told them they came from the 1904 World's Fair. Worth money, too. But they had no use for an incomplete set."

"The Louisiana Purchase Exposition," Hank says. "Fascinating. These are antiques, Chloe."

73

Antiques make her nervous. All that value placed on history that can't ever be corrected. Chloe feels Hank's foot nudge hers. She knows he wants her to handle the figures, somehow bond with them, not later, *right now*, in front of his parents. Of all the gifts these two have given her, Chloe feels this one tops them all. She places the box and figures in Hank's lap, excuses herself to go to the kitchen.

"I know it's my birthday," she says, opening the oven door, "but I went and baked a gingerbread anyway."

Iris makes noises about how she shouldn't have, but Chloe knows it's politeness. Deep down, the one thing Hank's parents admire about her is baking. Slicing the warm cake, she gets one of those involuntary shivers, and imagines the Chinese figures in the box. It is madness to feel so unsettled. Objects have no real power. She whips real cream with a small hand beater, adding two drops of Mexican vanilla at just the right time. Baking is like prayer, she thinks, you may not always like the answer you get, but at least you get one.

From the living room, she hears Hank laugh. It is a forced sound; he has a hard time with laughter these days. He is an untenured professor of folklore and mythology at a college where the air is thick with the talk of budget cuts. She places candles atop the cake. Not an accurate amount. Just enough to make a small fire. The exact date of her birthday was lost years ago in shuffling from care facilities to foster homes. During the seven years she stayed with the Gilpins, it was decided today would be a good day to celebrate her birthday. She has lived with Hank nine years, she realizes, longer than the Gilpins. It is the longest time she has stayed in any one place. She figures she is thirty-one years old.

"This girl has the touch," Charles says, pressing the tines of his fork into the crumbs on his plate.

Hank, mouth full, nods.

"Oh," Iris says, and presses her hand to her mouth.

"What is it, Mom? Are you in pain?"

She gives him a stern look. "Of course not. Possibly I have a loose filling. Hank, you hover over me every second."

Chloe can see Hank is wounded. An only child, born late in his parents' marriage, he worries about his mother constantly. He clips articles from health magazines and sends them to her. He presses the issue of cruciferous vegetables whenever they go out to eat. Chloe knows what would smooth this situation over is for her to fawn over the Chinese figures. To stroke the wooden limbs, the carved pigtails, to hook the lantern in the arm of the tall one, who seems to be smirking. Instead, she slices more cake, shrouds each piece with whipped cream and passes everyone a second helping.

When Iris and Charles leave, Chloe and Hank stand in the doorway and wave. Iris likes to wave back until they are out of sight. Charles concentrates his field of vision over the Oldsmobile's steering wheel, bumping into curbs, causing other drivers to honk and give him the finger.

"Well," Hank says. "Was that too awful?"

She takes a breath. "Since it's my birthday, I wonder if you would mind doing me this one teensy favor."

"I am not going to cater to your paranoia," Hank says. "They are wooden statues, like chessmen. Not an omen."

"I've never understood chess."

"You like the pieces. You like the knights. Those little horses. You'll learn to like these."

"From a distance? Like, say, the shelf in your office?"

Hank shakes his head. "Absolutely not. It's already too funereal in there."

In bed that night, Chloe presses her ear to Hank's chest. "I hear something," she says. "Not a galloping passion, mind you, but something in there."

"Go to sleep."

She unbuttons his pajamas. On her "birthday" he does not always give her a present, but they always make love. It is a tradition, the way some people, even as adults, still dress up for Halloween. Hank has one arm flung over his eyes, his sleeping posture. He pats her arm. "Listen, honey."

She gives his penis a little tap under the covers. "You're not that tired, Buster. You have a commitment here. Now wake up and fly right."

Hank groans.

"Now I get it," she says, still exploring with her fingers. "Possessed by the spirit of a dead Chinaman. But only in this one place."

"I'll give you possessed," he says.

"What a good idea," Chloe says. And this is how it begins.

Studying Hank by the streetlamp light coming through the window, Chloe runs her fingertips over his closed eyelids, bends and kisses. Beneath the skin, she can feel the lively flutter of each eye. She moves down the planes of his face, touching with her hands, lips, each new texture a stopping place. Hank smiles, pulls her to him. It is like diving into another medium, she thinks, one-third ocean, one-third earth and the last part unknown, like a dark cellar, where anything can happen. The phone rings and her limbs jump.

Both gasp and without having to ask, Chloe knows Hank's thinking: *my mother*. This is the phone call he awaits twenty-four hours a day. But as soon as his hand touches the receiver, the ringing stops. "Hello?" he says in the darkness, "hello," but no one's there. There is only the hum of the refrigerator (Chloe suspects the condenser coil is going) and a far-off siren, meant for someone else.

"Somebody realized they had misdialed," Hank says hopefully.

"Ha. It's the other Chinamen, calling their brothers. Please say you'll take them away."

"Be serious."

"I am."

"It's late. Go to sleep."

Cooling in the sheets, she wonders how it would be if she

started a fire. Just a small one. The guy with the lantern first. Then the one in the pill-box hat. He wears a hat, but goes barefoot. Lastly, the one with the gold-leaf slippers. If the figures could be destroyed without damaging anything of value, would anyone be hurt? Would Iris eat her vegetables? Charles willingly give up his driver's license? Would Hank roll over and finish what he started?

Ben Gilpin drove short hauls for Lucky markets and never missed church on Sundays. For a foster parent, he was considerate and gave Chloe her privacy. She discovered he was cheating on Margaret purely by accident. Her senior year, Chloe liked to cut Civics and Economics and walk to the bowling alley, where she would spend the afternoons smoking Sherman cigarettes and reading Gregory Corso. The alley was off-limits and therefore exceedingly attractive. Inside, she found Ben, his hair slicked back, wearing those funny rental shoes, rolling a tangerine-colored ball down the wooden alley. Alongside him, this dumpy blonde gave him little puckery fish-kisses every time he made his spare, and Chloe'd gone straight home, opened the *Joy of Cooking* and started in baking. Swedish rye bread, fat with molasses and fennel seed greeted Ben at supper time. Thereafter, Chloe baked weekly, as if food would fulfill a dual purpose — fill up Ben's needs, erase her terrible knowledge.

The Chinese figures see everything, despite their placement on the top shelf of her closet. They are not to be disposed of lightly, like the other gifts Iris and Charles have given her. The beige double-knit dress, that came from the rummage sale of Iris's dead neighbor. The country-style enamelware flower pot with the dangling rubber hoses that upon closer inspection appeared to be an antique, all right, an antique douching apparatus. No.

She and Hank laughed over those gifts. Think of something terrible, she would say. Now, imagine Charles and Iris as a magnetic field, and all this junk like iron filings. In the past, all those gifts marched to the Salvation Army like good little soldiers. But to send the Chinese brothers to strangers feels like leaving a

77

pet in the mountains. The guilt would return to haunt her. There is no possessing with these three, she decides, there is only being possessed.

Iris's voice on the telephone is soft, meandering over five different subjects before she says, "I don't want to bother Charles. Will you drive me to the doctor?"

Chloe is puzzled. These two have been Chang and Eng since Charles' retirement.

"There is just a little bleeding," Iris says, "but I'm sure it's nothing. So if you wouldn't mind."

In the waiting room, surrounded by mostly older folks with magazines and passive faces, Chloe thinks how she did not cry when Ben Gilpin died. It was quick, "an accident of the heart," Margaret called it. He'd gotten his gold watch from Lucky, his gold star in heaven for being a decent guardian to Chloe. He'd had luxury, too, his bowling alley flings she never disclosed and fifteen pounds gained on Chloe's cooking. I wonder if that killed him, she thinks, all that cholesterol in the butter. And sitting here in the clinic waiting room while Iris is being examined, hearing the syncopated turning of magazine pages — why, when there's time left, does anyone with cancer, *anyone*, care about movie stars' lives? — she is close to tears. As a child she learned not to give into tears. It is easier to bake; food is new even when the recipe is old. Set about to create something that cannot be stored, must be eaten or thrown out, is nourishing, and you are a little like a temporary god. And failing that, there's always sex, she thinks, and right there among the color-coordinated chairs and pamphlets on radiation therapy, she understands Ben Gilpin's affairs for the first time.

She'll bake Iris and Charles a casserole for supper. "Broccoli soldiers," from the Moosewood country cookbook. Broccoli is simple, good. Hank says *Rodale* lists it among the top three perfect foods.

Iris spends a few minutes with the receptionist, then turns to face Chloe. The turquoise comb that holds her hair has slipped to the side just a little. Time, with a capital T, her powdery cheeks say, it's just a matter of. Gently, Chloe takes her arm and together they walk to the car.

Sitting on the floor of the living room, Chloe examines the Chinese figures closely from where they stand on the coffee table. Gold Shoes has a hairline crack down his arm. It is glued together, she realizes. The lantern has a sloppy varnish job. The pillbox's proportions are wrong unless underneath the robe he is on stilts. She wonders how it is for them. If they miss the other members of the procession. Who they were burying. A leader, a lover? The possibilities are as endless as Ben Gilpin's bowling alley beauties. She imagines needing the kind of duplistic lovemaking where the mind travels independent of the body. That's not immoral. Hell, it's being honest.

A peach pie with a fluted crust, oozing amber glaze. Two loaves of French bread shellacked with egg white. A tin of brownies that contain enough fudge to fell an Easter rabbit. The goodies cause the kitchen counter to sag under a fattening perfume that invades every room of the house.

"I am quitting teaching," Hank announces in the doorway.

"Why this time?"

He kisses her neck. "I stopped for gas on the way home and the guy at the Texaco seemed to have a great little deal going. Hell, he doesn't even have to put the nozzle in the hole anymore. Just takes the money. He doesn't have to sit on pins through departmental meetings at the bitch factory, that's for sure."

"You don't understand cars. Besides, you love the bitch factory."

"I do?"

"You'd confuse the customers at the gas station telling them Zeus was inside their carburetor."

"Probably. But I was thinking: Prometheus Gas and Oil. Has a ring to it."

It's hot in the kitchen, and Chloe watches as Hank strips off his jacket, tie, rolls up the sleeves of the blue oxford cloth shirt she ironed this morning. "Your mother's having some bleeding, Hank. I drove her to the doctor and she asked me not to tell you."

He sits down on the couch. "Define 'some.'"

"She didn't say, but I think they want her to go back in the hospital."

Hank pours himself a Glenfiddich. He is a scholar, even when it comes to drinking. Small sips, lots of staring, no food to distract the act. Chloe leaves him alone.

"Wake up," he tells her.

"What now?"

Hank drags her to the living room, where he has obviously spent the evening with the scotch. There are three squares of tin foil spread out on the floor and atop each one, a Chinese figure. He wraps them carefully, like ears of corn for the barbeque, then takes her hand and leads her outside to the backyard.

He makes her sit down in front of a hole he has dug. He curls himself around her back, so that she is wearing him like a shell. Resting his head on her shoulder, he tells her in a low voice, "When I was a kid, I was in love with ritual. The trappings, the pomp. For a while I thought I wanted to be a priest."

"I'm grateful that didn't last."

"No, you have to listen. It was different for you. I know you missed a lot of this. There were all these fairs when I was a kid. For a dime's worth of effort, you could win anything. I wasn't terribly coordinated. I must have spent close to twenty bucks throwing ping-pong balls into fishbowls before I ever won my first fish. I had hope for those fish. I would think of an undefeatable name for the little bastard, like Spartacus, but the next morning, I'd find him belly up. It happened every time."

"I'm sorry, Hank. Do you want to get an aquarium?"

He laughs. "You misunderstand. I'm just showing you what the beauty of it was. Funerals." He moves toward the foil-wrapped figures, glinting like bars of silver. "First, you must wrap them in tin-foil, and it has to be close to midnight. That's very important. You make a marker out of stones or sticks. And say a prayer."

"Does it matter which one? I don't know a lot of prayers."

He waves his hand. "It's not important. You can do that part after."

With his hands over hers, he places the figures in the hole and tamps the earth down, setting the rocks in place.

"Now what?"

"That's it. Then one year later, you dig them up and examine the bones."

This is what I missed? Oh, Ben Gilpin, where is the freedom in this? She wonders what is possibly left to bake, what recipe she hasn't yet tried that will staunch the tears beginning to flood Hank's eyes.

Then Hank, who has up until now always been shy about such matters, slides her nightgown to the ground and begins something right there in the backyard with only the streetlight for a witness. This time, his hands promise, whatever they start, he'll finish.

CAKE WALK

for C.J.

We spent a languorous summer in southern California, a mile from the beach, slouched in the dark on a half-paid-for couch drinking vodka mixed with powdered lemonade crystals left over from some camping trip. I figured it was about as tropical as two girls could get in a rented apartment, waiting out the dark, convinced if we got sarcastic and potted, the sky would give up and get light on us.

I drank to keep my sister Rory company. She was unemployed; I was working the day shift at Weldon's. We couldn't afford cable, so watching TV was really dragging the lake, but drinking made it tolerable. We kept the room dark, the screen and the street lamp our only source of light. At any moment you could look up and see the shadow of the cypress tree outside magnified on the ceiling, slowly swishing through this cathode wash of green, blue, pink.

Rory's bruises were at the yellow healing stage and they'd caught the guy who'd assaulted her. Is that a nice way of saying rape? I'd asked the social services woman they'd sent around with the identifying photographs — *Alleged*, she'd reminded me, nothing's been proven in court yet. But they caught the guy, so things were looking up. Now Rory would almost smile at me before she lifted her first drink of the night to the stitched-up lip. I made clever toasts and narrated the television screen antics.

We watched it all: Mr. Ed, in his fruits-and-vegetables hat dancing like Carmen Miranda; Dr. Gene Scott scrawling magic marker pyramids of Armageddon; reruns of *The Philadelphia Story* and *Pat and Mike*.

"Will you look at that damn Katherine Hepburn," I'd whisper, my ice cubes dwindling against the glass, melting from the heat of my hand. "Who needs her cheekbones? Why, I'll bet if she snuggled up to Spencer Tracy, she could give him a shave."

Rory's heart-shaped face rested on her hands. I kidded her. "Aurora Jean! You're not listening! Rory, remember in school how Mrs. Sims would get all hiked up calling out 'Aurora Jean!' You know what I think, I think she just liked the way your name rolled off her tongue. Oh, God, do you remember that time you let the classroom lizards go, how that one went up Susan Miller's dress and she peed right on the spot? She deserved it, calling us orphans."

Rory the silent sister. Rory the mute. Elbows and knees and all the best throw pillows.

"If you recall, Aurora Jean, I didn't tell, even though I ended up taking the whipping for it. Wouldn't you say, if someone were taking a survey or something, wouldn't you say I'm not just good, I'm somewhat *excellent* at keeping secrets?"

She was quiet. It was what I imagined living with a completely paralyzed person was like.

For three weeks she'd worn a blue kimono I'd bought on a remainder rack in Chinatown. There was a dragon embroidered over her left breast and a bleach stain at either wrist.

"The tie for it's in the bathroom," I said. "Don't you at least want it belted?" She didn't answer.

I kept busy. I made up an excellent recipe for peach goo to put on top of ice cream, altering the family recipe for jam. First, you peel the peaches, because having that hairy globular skin in your mouth is worse than having to kiss — what? Monkey butts? Add lemon juice and sugar; stir. Spoon it on Thrifty's vanilla ice cream and pretend it is something your grandmother won first prize for at a county fair. Smile like girls who have been raised on slow-cooking Quaker Oats and real icicles. Eat like there's no tomorrow.

And Rory ate whatever I fixed her. I worked my eight-hour shift, came home and scraped the grated onions out of my tennis shoe treads. She stayed at home all day and took showers. We settled in on the couch and did completely regular things. I painted her toenails Dune Damask, fixed her snacks of canned shoestring potatoes and Durkee's French-fried onion rings. I even answered my own questions so she could rest her healing lip. If we'd had a mother she would have called us every night.

But in the wee hours, when TV kind of exhausted itself, right before the travel advisories came on, I would wonder if Rory and I weren't just a little bit like Norman and his mother up at the Bates motel.

It wasn't morbid curiosity, but the thing was, Rory didn't talk to anyone about what had actually happened. Our imaginary Mom would have said she Didn't Care to Know the Details and I guess the doctors in the emergency room had enough evidence to refute the *alleged*, but there was the element of my sister unburdening herself. I hoped it would happen soon.

It had made us unnaturally introspective, I suppose, being brought up by old people, and maybe a little world-worried to boot. Here it was summer, but I was remembering when Grampy was still alive, all that sentimental business at Thanksgiving over enough food for ten families, let alone the four of us staring down at the overflowing wicker cornucopia. He was a sharp old coot, utterly in fear of current politics, and every year he chose Thanksgiving as the occasion to explain step-by-step how the Domino theory was coming true from way before Viet Nam to Afghanistan to whatever it is the Ayatollah is up to these days.

He'd wave the serving fork. "Today Cambodia, tomorrow Philadelphia! They like those places that end in vowels!"

"Eat your yams," Grammy'd say to him, and before he minded her, he'd drag out the heavy artillery: the spelling.

"A-l-b-a-n-i-a, R-o-m-a-n-i-a, C-z-e-c-h-o-s-l-o-v-a-k-i-a..." Then he'd eat, getting marshmallow and orange sticky grukka all over his moustache, but by then Rory and I would be struck dumb. We weren't stupid — A-m-e-r-i-c-a, Ca-l-i-f-o-r-n-i-a.

"Look what you've done to the girls," Grammy would holler and I'd start blubbering. Then she'd whisk out the dessert even though we had never even tasted the turkey and what did Grampy care? He just went on nodding in between mushy bites because he knew he was right. And Rory and I would stare at each other, trembling under our good dresses, hungry enough to seriously consider trying the wax fruit.

The night the TV blew up we were watching *Hawaii-Five-O* and I was watching especially close because I was sure this was going to be the time I would get to see Dan-o 'book 'em' on camera, but ping! the picture tube just went and sealed itself into a green dot and the living room smelled of burning circuits.

"Russians," I said, mostly to myself, but then I figured between Rory and me we had just watched that old Sony to a premature death. It was still early, quarter past nine, a baby of a night and because the TV was off we could suddenly hear the not-too-distant sounds of the local county fair, the desperate attempts of an aged surf band trying for a comeback.

"This is it, Rory," I said. "Pink cotton candy. The trained poodle act. The amazing Ginszu knife that saws through a beer can and still produces paper-thin tomato slices. We're going."

I dressed her in my Weldon's turquoise-and-cantaloupe jumpsuit and dragged her to the car, tumbler of vodka and lemonade crystals right along with her. We were lucky that the Volvo started up without the usual incantations, and who knew, before the night was over, we might draw the lucky ticket stub that would win us a Brand New Car!

All Rory wanted to do besides feed her cotton candy to the miniature horse was the cake walk.

"Come on. Nobody wins at that," I scoffed, "and besides, we'd have to carry the cake around all night. Let's make a killing at the dime-toss. Lose our lunch on the loop-de-loop. Do something memorable."

"It reminds me of my childhood," she uttered, a phrase I suspected she'd memorized from one of innumerable black-and-white movies we'd watched, but it was her first actual sentence in weeks, so cake walk it was.

An old lady in an eyepatch was staring at us, tugging at her double-knit. You had to be over forty to cakewalk right. Then a scary guy wearing a sleeveless T-shirt who was in charge of the music let it rip, and when it stopped Rory's bedroom slippers were standing on the winning number.

"Sweet thing, you just go on and take your pick," he told my sister, and Rory went for the pink peppermint job like she knew it was hers all along. She just stood there holding it in her hands like this was the moment you wait for all your life.

Then her face went slack and her lips started moving, but they had started another cakewalk and the hurdy-gurdy music was yammering right in my ear. So whatever she was saying was lost in the medley.

I took her over by the Araucana chickens that lay colored eggs and asked her please could she repeat it again.

Those clear monofilaments that were her stitches curled back against her teeth like baby walrus whiskers and she talked for a solid ten minutes just holding that cake.

"He said, 'Bitch. I'm going to redefine the meaning of the word.' And tied me up in my own bathrobe belt, Rickie. And then he kissed me on the mouth like it was our first date. I'm not saying it wasn't bad, Rickie. It was worse than anything that could follow." Her hand holding the cake shook but she wasn't going to cry, no sir. "You know what?"

"What?"

"Sometimes when we're watching TV, I can almost forget the other stuff ever happened. And how everything took so long. But it's his mouth I can't erase. I see it over and over. I've scrubbed myself raw and I can't get it off me." She gave me a half-grin. "Not even with Zest."

She scuffed her slipper toes on the asphalt and I knew it was time. It was up to me to plant some seed that would bring her back, if not now, then maybe in the future. The metallic whine of the bobsled ride rocked the night air. There was nothing to say, but I started talking, hoping the words would come to me as I went along.

"There's more than one kind."

Rory shot me a look.

I took a breath. "I think men are somewhat necessary, Rory. Who'd open jars for us? Think of it, being trapped in the kitchen, unable to crack the vacuum lock on the Planter's party mix. And there's geography. Who else can tell you where the strait of *Hormuz* is? The Beatles were men; I guess they still are. I don't know. I think the main thing is not to close your heart."

Rory had her eyes shut, but she was listening, which kind of surprised me, because as usual, I was talking too much about nothing. I wished I could give her a sisterly hug just then, but the cake was preventing us from getting really close and all when the old grinch with the eyepatch came forward and tapped Rory on the shoulder.

"Excuse me," she said, "but I see you haven't tasted your cake yet and I was just wondering if I could tempt you into trading it for, say, this Tunnel of Fudge. See, my Mister's had his eye on that one all night and he has a sweet tooth for peppermint."

Rory handed her the cake.

"This means a lot," the lady said. "He'll be tickled."

"Great," I said. "Glad to help."

Rory started to cry. "Crumb, Rickie. Is that it?"

I put my arm around her. "Honey, it's all I know."

Right there in the dark with the hot, sticky gum and half-eaten hamburger bun smells of the fair she wailed out loud — a troubled soul. I was shocked, but managed a groan in comeback. All the old cakewalkers gave us bad looks, but what did we care? She set the cake down and we hugged, sisters, the same two girls we would be at forty, sixty and even way after that, when we were tucked well under the earth.

We sat in the car and sliced pieces off that fudge cake until it was a mess of crumbles and our blood sugars were somewhere in the quadruplebillions. The parking lot emptied before we were done talking and we sat there staring at this strange color in the sky. Rory thought it might be a planet you could only see in late summer and I was thinking possibly UFOs-Russians. But it turned out to be only the sun, coming up.

THE GREENBROKE SISTERS: Lillie and Rose

OWNING THE VIEW

The nurse opens the curtains in the private room, the only one left on the crowded ward. Rose can see the ocean from the window — Catalina centered in the distance — a postcard view. No doubt islanders are strolling in the February sun, eating junk food, watching fish from the glass-bottomed boats. Not standing here vacillating over fifty extra dollars a night.

"Some view," the nurse says.

"It's lovely," Rose says. "But I seriously doubt Blue Cross is going to think it's lovelier than sharing a four-bed ward."

The nurse — her name plate reads Connie, though she looks too businesslike and too old to have a name ending in IE — presses further.

"Up on sixth, where all the celebs stay, you'd pay through the nose. Here, it's just an architectural accident. But don't listen to me. Wait until the sun sets. Then it speaks for itself. You're lucky to be here, Rose."

Rose offers her arm for blood pressure.

"Jewelry? Eyeglasses? A wedding ring? The hospital maintains a safe for valuables on the lobby floor."

"Just contact lenses."

"You want to give them to me now?"

"Not a chance," Rose says. "Not only am I half-blind without them, I'd miss my view."

Connie leans back, playing with the snap mechanism on the clipboard. "Would you like a Valium? Dr. Pedersen said you could have one."

91

Rose nods without really thinking. Why the hell not? If it doesn't help the time pass, it will insulate it.

Connie fluffs her pillows. "How about a cup of tea? It's herbal. No caffeine."

"Thanks. Maybe later." Rose knows it's her face that gives her nerves away. All her life it's been so. There's something unfair about having the complexion of a redhead. The emotions filter through, like the blush on a peach.

"Keep it in mind. We keep the water on twenty-four hours."

When Connie finally leaves the room, satisfied with her quota of answers to chart, Rose gets up from the bed and investigates. Starting with the window.

It's a corner window. Two walls of plate glass that reveal the Pacific. All steel-blues and bottle glass greens because this is the tail end of February, winter in southern California. The Valium cushions the edges just a little. It's a delicious feeling watching the water when she should be at work. She almost forgets why she's in the hospital in the first place.

Her watch blinks 4:30. Still too early for her sister to arrive. In an abbreviated phone call between meetings, Rose explained her test results, the change in schedule for the surgery.

"He wants to do it tomorrow morning. I guess so he doesn't miss his golf date."

"Good," Lillie'd said. "Get the whole business over with."

It is sisterly concern to the extent Lillie can muster. She doesn't like anticipating the inevitable. Tonight she'll probably suggest they watch game shows and make fun of the contestants. Or try on spring shades of eyeshadow. Anything to avoid the subject at hand.

But even if asked point blank, Rose doesn't feel right talking to Lillie about the hysterectomy. What it means, how even Valium fails to unknot the loss. There's a protocol to their relationship. Lillie, twenty-five to her thirty-four, is still in the position of needing counsel. Rose is the only one left to provide it.

Three years back when their mother died, Lillie became stony, full of a quiet anger she denied. Then she started in with

92

this attitude, as if confronting the death of one parent and the abandonment of another in one lifetime was just one more piece of evidence that she was put on earth to party. Underneath the mini-skirts, the smart-ass banter, Lillie grieves. And because Rose has her own set of griefs, she understands her sister, compelled to own six pair of cowboy boots and always craving the latest style just set in the window.

Six years back, when Rose was still married to Phil, racking the anniversaries up to everyone's astonishment, she remembers how she behaved like a neutered cat. Too stupidly content to work at keeping that happiness. She shakes her head at such an ironic image. The Valium? She looks at the water.

If Lillie were here, she would point to the island and tell about when she was a kid, camping with the Girl Scouts. How the wild pigs ate their hobo soup and makings for *S'mores*, forcing the leaders to take eighteen Brownies to a swanky nightclub for supper. That kind of thing. But the sunset will be gone by the time she arrives, the light slipping toward the other side of the globe. This isn't self-pity. It is simply the way her life is constructed that she is alone most of time. The giver, the consoler. Necessary roles. Even at the art gallery where she is assistant manager, people seem to need her more often than she needs them.

At the creak of the door behind her, she expects Connie, wanting to repeat a blood pressure or to hand her that promised cup of tea. But it's not her. A doctor.

"I'm home again, Rose," he sings. "Remember in the Music Man when the barbershop quartet sang 'Lydah Rose?' God, what a great tune. Now I won't be able to get it out of my head for days. I never met a girl named Lydah. And you're my first Rose this spring. Is that short for anything?"

"Rose Maxwell."

It's an annoying habit the staff has — starting conversations in the middle, calling everyone by their first names — as if they're old buddies. It makes her feel among other things, too young to be having the hysterectomy. She watches him fiddle through the multiplying pages of her file.

His tan is careful, even. Body straight out of the *Sharper Image* home gym set. The lines that appear in his face as he smiles are accidental, as if he caught them crewing his way down to Cabo. The gray hair is an inch too long at the collar line. Divorced or widowed, she guesses. Wonders if he has any daughters.

"I don't mean to be rude, but who are you?"

"Sorry. I'm the gas man. Here to send you to la-la land in the morning. I've got a whole page here of terrible consequences I'm supposed to read to you. But I'd just as soon skip it. Frankly, they'll scare you to death." He pauses for emphasis. "But it's up to you. I can read them if you want."

"Pass," she says, grateful for Valium, making it easy to smile at anything. Her tongue is a rubber band. "I'm scared enough. Talk about consequences. As of tomorrow, my bikini retires."

He arches an eyebrow. "From what I hear, you're getting off pretty easy."

"So they tell me. If nothing's spread, I get to keep one ovary. Why do I keep thinking that sounds like a bad Yahtzee score?"

He laughs too loud, then scribbles on a page in her folder. "I'm just going to write you an order for a sleeping pill. Now don't worry. You'll get plenty of shut-eye. This will be over with before you know it." He gives her a wink. He looks like somebody's grandpa when he's being himself.

If he'd just go, she could resume staring at the ocean again. It's changing without her. Getting darker. If she has to make any more conversation, she'll miss the sunset. Sunsets in California are a dime a dozen. But this one seems precious. More important than etiquette. She's paying extra for it. With her checkbook and her womb.

"So. We have a date for the morning?"

Such an earnest face. Lillie would say something smart-ass. But she's not Lillie.

She nods. He leaves. There it is. Her sunset, a tomcat's whisker of orange bisecting the two grays. Like a Meyer-Gaster watercolor bleeding into the sea from a top-heavy sky. She stares out long after it's gone, her last viable sunset with all the parts intact.

* * *

"Here to prep you." A young girl in a white lab coat plops down a green plastic basket that looks as if it belongs inside someone's dishwasher full of dirty knives and spoons, not holding test tubes and bandages.

"You want to come get back in bed so we can get it over with?"

"I understood I could keep everything till morning."

But the girl has already ripped open her Betadine scrubs and peeled the wrapper back from a disposable razor. "Your surgery's scheduled for 6:15 A.M. It'll save hassles if we just do this now."

The businesslike hands quickly lift her gown and place warmed towels above and below her pubic hair.

"I hope you get paid decent money to do this."

"It's no big deal. I lucked out, really. So far nobody on this floor's needed a diaper change and you're the only pre-op gyney I drew. I go home in twenty minutes."

She hears in the girl's tone that she's overstepped some kind of invisible boundary. That what she should be doing is averting her eyes while she is stripped of the soft brown hair that has been part of her identity since she was twelve years old. The razor scritches as it is drawn over her skin. The second the flesh is exposed, it puckers. Gooseflesh.

"We're in the middle of a procedure," her technician calls out at a knock at the door. "So just hang on a minute."

"I'll just bet," Rose hears Lillie yell from behind the door. "Step on it, will you? I've got a couple procedures here myself and they're getting cold."

The tech swears softly under her breath. She's in a hurry to leave now, gathering her goodies into the basket. In her haste, she forgets the square of gauze that holds the clippings of hair.

Rose folds it in two, tucking it under the telephone on the night-stand. Later, she'll have to remember to throw it away.

Then the door flies open. Everyone: not just Lillie (who gives the departing lab coat a suspicious look), but most of her staff from the gallery as well. Jenny, sporting a swollen lower lip, inspires a kind of Pia Zadora vulnerability. God knows what sort of flap she's been in. Maybe it's simply pouting, or she's forgotten her Zovirax. Hank sets one of his wooden horses at the foot of the bed.

"Present," he says. "Limited edition."

Ted, Rose's boss, is arm in arm with Sharon, looking so expectant this might be a last-minute dinner party. And there's someone Rose doesn't recognize. He could be an entanglement of Jenny's, or knowing Lillie, someone she met in the elevator and found interesting. He smiles.

Rose turns a hot shade of pink all the way down underneath her gown, as if he can see her pubic region, newly bald as a baby eagle.

"So," Lillie says. "We're stranded out in the hall feeling sorry for you. Meanwhile, you're doing procedures with young girls."

"Don't you think six visitors at a time might be bending the rules just a little?"

"Relax. If anyone gets excited, we'll just send people in shifts to visit the other patients. Fair and square," Lillie says.

Rose bites her lip and tries to telepathically shoot her sister a thank you. Lillie's trying her best. She must be terrified. Out of Jenny's saddlebag purse comes a Calzone and a bottle of Chateau Margaux. Sharon unwraps a plate of pate studded with what look like broccoli soldiers.

They pace her room as if they are on a carefully planked deck overlooking Emerald Bay instead of four stories up on the crotch ward.

Rose shakes her head. "You guys. You know I can't eat. I have surgery in the morning."

Hank moves the sculptured horse closer. "No problem.

Chester'll keep you company. He's a little off his feed lately. Your sister's been using him as a rack to dry her underwear."

Lillie deliberately crosses the room.

"Careful, Hank. Lillie doesn't like that kind of thing said out loud."

"I'm tired of being careful. Either she lives with me or she doesn't. What am I? Some temporary hangar she can tie down to when she feels like it?"

Rose smoothes a frayed thread at the cuff of his cowboy shirt. "You know what Chester thinks?"

"Chester's full of horseshit."

"He knows he'd rather be Lillie's underwear rack than just one of the herd."

He stares past her to Lillie. "God, that's so deep. Write it down, will you?"

Ted waves the Pentax. "Come on, Rose. Your best Camille."

She places the knuckles of her right hand against her forehead. "How's this?"

Lillie's stranger takes her arm, gently. "Camille's been done to death. Try 'Mrs. Siddons as a Tragic Muse.' A little more arch in your back. You've got the arms right."

"Now this is one hell of a picture," Ted says.

Jenny's a little drunk. "Look at this place. Room's nicer than my apartment. Than the whole complex. Aw, Christ. will you all check out the view? Move over, you just got yourself a roommate."

"One night here will cost you rnore than just a month's rent, sugar. They take all sorts of indecent liberties with you."

"Poor Jenny," Ted says, snapping her pout. "Get Hank to set you up with Chester. He's plenty indecent."

Elsewhere, Lillie's laugh suddenly fills the room. It spills and leaks all over the place, stopping everyone for a minute. Rose knows it well. It never occurs to Lillie to tidy up the guffaws or make it businesslike. By the window, filling her face with the last of the Calzone, Lillie seems loose-reined as a horse that's just dumped his rider. She's chatting with the Tragic Muse, but he's looking over her head, winking. Things seem to be heating up everywhere. Then Connie appears with her styrofoam cup of tea.

Ted photographs her standing in the doorway. It's a classic warden's pose. Her free hand on her hip, right foot poised for stamping an end to all this frivolity.

"Miss Maxwell. If you ate anything we'll have to cancel your surgery. You're aware of that?"

"I didn't eat a thing, honestly. They meant well. I suspect they didn't want me to be alone. Don't be too hard on them. They're all I've got."

"Well, they'll have to go. They're breaking just about all the rules. There's a patient next door who just lost a baby. I'm sure she'd appreciate a little peace."

Everyone's quiet. Sharon starts picking up their litter. Ted puts the Pentax back into its case. Lillie looks as if she doesn't know quite what to do. One hand is pressed against the glass of the lucky window as if she wants out.

"Oh, for Christ's sake," the Tragic Muse says. "We're sorry about the lady next door. But no one meant any harm. This is Southern California, for crying out loud. A party's required pre-operative care. Your hospital politics are a smokescreen, sugar. So can the righteousness trip."

Connie squares off, pointing a finger at his beard. She backs him up a few paces with the stubby finger. "Now you just hold your horses. This may be nothing but a So-Cal soiree to you, Mr. Party Animal. But it's a business to me. I can appreciate that you wanted to impress your girlfriend with your little diatribe. I can also appreciate that you have about five minutes to clear every-one out of this room so she can get some sleep. What you do out-side of here is none of my concern. But you don't dick around with major surgery. Do we understand each other?"

"Mr. Party Animal?" Jenny whispers.

He crosses the room to Rose's bed, leans down, takes her in his arms and kisses her.

Rose keeps her eyes open. This is a movies-type of kiss. The mouth opens wide, but nothing more than a quick dart of the tongue's involved. More defiant than tender. Like he knew he could get away with it. She can smell the wine on his breath and hear somebody's gasp (probably Jenny's jealous) and Lillie's laugh start all over again before the rest of them start hooting and clapping.

When they break apart, he falters, catching himself on the nightstand. He points at Connie. "Take that and put it in one of your stainless steel bedpans and smoke it," he says. Then leaves, shutting the door very quietly behind him.

"Very original." She stations herself at the door, propping it open with one foot. Clearly the kiss has cost them the last five minutes.

Rose is left alone with Lillie sitting Indian-style on the foot of her bed. "My sister," she says. "She'll behave. You have my word."

"Ten minutes. Then you have your sleeping pill."

"I don't think I'll need one."

"You'll need it."

When she's gone, Rose turns off all the lights except the spot over the sink in her private bathroom. The room feels cavernous with just the two of them on the bed. The lucky window has gone the color of the birds dotting the lawn of the state college. Purple-black, almost oily. Far down the highway, headlights are coming on. Hank's truck will be among them, driving Jenny home. Rose imagines the requisite pawing she'll give him at her front door and how tactfully he'll disentangle. Lillie snuffles and wipes her nose on the hem of her skirt.

"Why the tears? It was a wonderful surprise. Even if I couldn't eat a thing. You guys make me feel loved."

"Face it, Rose. I suck at planning details. Your nurse is a big help. Who does she think she is? Her hairdo reminds me of Haille Selassie."

Rose laughs. "She was just trying to do her job."

"A Nazi. I should have guessed by the rubber shoes."

"You want to know my favorite part?"

Lillie snuggles down into the covers at the foot of the bed. "Jenny's mouth? I love how she tries to pass off those whoppers as bumping into walls. If she's going to date such meatballs, you'd think she'd learn to duck."

"Speaking of lips. Where did you find that guy? He kisses like an actor."

"He was hanging around the gallery. I thought you knew him. Why? Interested?"

"Let's just say he made an impression."

"Come on, Rose. The beard. The little speech against authority. Moored in the late sixties. I know you love that sort of thing."

"Could I at least have the sheet? I'm paying for this."

"All right. What'd I say?"

"Nothing. Aren't I entitled to a crappy mood?"

"Apparently you think so."

"It's stupid. Phil had a beard. That guy kissing me just made me remember."

"Rose?" Lillie sounds about eight years old. "Are you okay? Not about the surgery. That'll go fine. I mean about not being able to have babies any more."

The words heave down on her chest, a solid weight Valium and the party cannot ease away. She squints in the dark, trying to see in her mind that old view of herself — twenty years from now, part of a family portrait that includes three generations. But that will never be. Instead, what she imagines duplicates this very moment — herself and Lillie, old ladies, still chattering in the dark on a twin bed.

Maybe it's generational. All through college there were free clinics. Everyone she knew became quite adept at avoiding pregnancy, as if they were juggling their eggs, and could keep them all in the air at the same time. For years. Now every magazine she picks up has articles on in-vitro fertilization and her own little plum: endometriosis.

She sighs. Lillie leans over and puts her head in Rose's lap. Rose strokes the long red hair, pulling combs free until the weight of her hair rests in her hands. It's thick stuff, stubborn and wiry. Her own neck-length waves seem paler, and behind her left ear, secret gray hairs have begun to sprout. When she crushes Lillie's hair, there is resilience, almost an echo of her laugh.

"It just hits me once in a while. Too bad I'm not more like you. Enough of this looking back at what can't be changed. Not that I'd have made such a great mother, anyway."

"You're a rotten sister."

She curls the hair around her wrist. "Just having the choice. You know."

"Here's a promise. If I ever have kids, I'll give you all the girls to raise. They're such pains. Who needs them?"

They're quiet, each touching the other's hand lightly. Both faces damp with tears they pretend not to notice. Lillie sits up and wipes her eyes, bends forward and French-braids her hair, glancing at the window for a mirror.

"You don't have to come back in the morning. I'll be all drugged out. You can call me in the afternoon. But don't take time off work special. Promise."

"I don't make promises. But the next party I throw in your honor, I'll invite only guys with beards who still have all their old Beatle records. Beyond that, can I bring you anything?"

"A wig for my nether regions. You should see what that technician did to me." She leans over to the nightstand to fetch the gauze square. It's gone. "Lillie. What was the name of the guy who kissed me?"

"Christ, I don't remember. What's the big deal anyway?"

"I think he stole my pubic hair."

Lillie's laugh helps fill the empty spaces. It seems like the funniest thing in the world — that guy with Rose's hair tucked into his change pocket. It spurs them on until the tears reduce to something altogether different.

"God," Lillie says. "I'm getting snot all over this skirt. Well, I suppose one way to look at it is he wanted something to remember you by. I guess you impressed him."

"I hate to think what else it could mean."

"Don't worry. Knowing your friends, it'll probably turn up in a piece of sculpture."

"That's exactly what worries me."

"Stop worrying. Kiss me goodnight. Get some rest."

Her sister's exit is swift. The skirt rustles, the door shuts silently. Connie appears with the sleeping pill and stands by the bed until Rose swallows it.

"Could you leave the curtains open?" she asks.

"There's really nothing to see."

"Please?"

The window provides enough light for removing her contact lenses. She floats them in individual pools in the case on the nightstand. The nurse is wrong; the view may not be specific, but something is there. The lights stream together like time-lapse photography. Even reduced to that, it stirs something in her, allowing the memories of Phil to surface.

* * *

Meeting in San Francisco in the mid-sixties, then breaking up just a few weeks after that woman tried to shoot Gerald Ford. Were they were always in the middle of something political, crazy? Phil said the important thing was to continue growing in all directions. Leave options open. Let the empty spaces fill in themselves. Sort of an echo of the architecture he was studying. Rose, happy, agreeing with him, stuck pretty much to a linear path, satisfied with her corner view of the park, where on her way back from the market, she could see the horseback riders cooling down their mounts. She admired the geodesic domes and passive solar gain dugouts Phil planned for the Berkeley hills, but Frank Lloyd Wright he wasn't.

At the end, everything she did seemed to irritate him. He'd criticize the arrangement of her textbooks on the pine and cinder-block shelves. Push his favorite chicken and rice dish aside as if it were camp food. When he'd started in on the color of the cat's flea collar, she'd cornered him.

"They only come in blue," she'd said. "If you're seeing someone, just tell me."

"The trouble here," and she remembers distinctly how his arm made a sweeping gesture, altering the contents of the third floor apartment they'd carefully restored to San Francisco primeval. The carefully stripped oak had gone bare, the white walls no longer pristine, were one-dimensional. "The trouble here is we're too much like friends. Best friends."

Granted, their lovemaking had become a little slower, kind of like a glorified hugging. But that didn't necessarily mean an end to passion. She went to him, put her arms around his shoulders and felt the distance. All her life, embracing had been instrumental, a specific barometer of the truth. Her mother's terse flexing, which contained a lifetime of pain endured to raise two girls without a father. Lillie's spontaneous mugging, (thanks for a new goldfish when the cat had dined on the old one). Phil's arms had encircled more than her body; tucked in between them had been the fat ghosts of future possibilities — children. She put the cat's collar into the junk drawer and shed her tears in the bathroom. Together they sat at the kitchen table and figured out what half their various savings accounts amounted to. Phil kept looking up and smiling. He packed cheerfully and right up to the moment when he handed her his set of house keys, she honestly believed he would recant, blaming his behavior on a phase of the moon. Some lunar idiocy he would beg her to forget.

But Phil went. And three weeks later, when the mid-cycle cramping sent her to the clinic, there was a surprise.

"This will not be a viable pregnancy," the embarrassed doctor explained to her knees, scheduling her D and C, quickly emphasizing it was not the same thing as an abortion with the spotting and the pain factor.

"It simply wasn't meant to be."

"To hell with San Francisco," Lillie's letter had said. "Quake bait. Who wants to live in a town just waiting to fall down again? Not to mention those guys down on Market Street. Come back to the Southland, Rose. We'll surf Thirty-eighth Street with the locals. Eat Mom's pot roast and let her iron our good blouses. Get tans you could die for."

She went and Lillie had been right. From the second she looked out of the window of the plane, turning her back on the bay, the view seemed warmer, more inviting. The pot roast put meat on her bones. The job at the gallery was fulfilling. But only Lillie knows this — no one to warm her feet on for the last seven years.

* * *

The sleeping pill is starting to work. She fights, feeling the drug pull at her as if she is being tied into a mummy sleeping bag. She arches her neck to focus in the direction of the lucky window.

When she wakes up first thing in the morning, it will offer one of those typical southern California brilliancies. The sea almost painfully blue. Or it might be cloudy, overcast, a calm hammered silver that wants polishing. Somewhere along the edge of all that brightness, a bearded thief walks around with her pubic hair. If Hank were to frame it — in something exotic, like *padouk* — she bets there isn't one person in the world who wouldn't give up something vital and precious just to claim they own it.

HOOFBEATS

Barrett is sleeping. Earlier, at the opening for the minimalist series by Perras, he went hog-wild on the guacamole dip. Rose, lying next to him, knows the liberal use of onion is what made his stomach knot up, and why he had to take one of those pills that knock him out for the entire night. She knows it isn't her place to lecture him on the merits of such trade-offs. Enough times she has seen him falter in front of hot dog stands or confronting a bowl of Charlie's chili weighing his alternatives.

She almost admires the kind of inner strength it takes to invite a bout of gastritis for a brief indulgence. But if Barrett woke up, she wouldn't tell him. Or even ask what that last phone call from Sybil was about. She would just ask him to rub her leg, because it is aching again.

The pain is not constant. It comes and goes. Goes whenever things are progressing in their lives and the days spent together seem light, full of promise, like the day they signed the papers on the gallery. Their signatures on the agreement were distinct and individual, but both slanted the same way. Then it comes when she is this tired but finds sleep impossible, and lies there wondering. There is Sybil (who used to be married to Barrett), her phone calls seeking Albert's (their son) return. There is Barrett. If he weren't sleeping off the guacamole, he would find time to rub her leg. He uses his fingertips in small circles and tells Rose she doesn't warm up properly before exercise. This is as good an explanation as any, but Rose suspects it is not the reason for the pain. She hopes it will go away the same way it came.

Ignoring it is like keeping her mouth shut when she realized Barrett was not planning to return Albert. It was the first time since he'd moved in with Rose that Sybil had agreed to a visit. Things were so touchy, they met in the desert, a hundred miles from anywhere, as if it were the DMZ. About the same time the calls from Sybil began (Barrett sneaking the receiver into the closet where he could yell without Albert hearing), the pain in her leg developed. Now that the calls are few, the phone cord hanging politely down the wall, the pain should diminish, but it has not. Puzzles and changes, Rose thinks. Does Sybil like life better without her son?

As if he can plug into these thoughts, Albert appears at the bedside. Rose senses the blue eyes boring into her face, the silent sentinel Albert is becoming when they hold these late-night discussions.

"Albert's awake," she whispers to Barrett's back.

He answers in German. *"Was ist diene namme, madschen?"*

He thinks that's funny because he speaks it and she doesn't. He could be conjugating verbs or cursing raw onion for all she knows. He isn't waking up to see to Albert.

"Rose?" Albert whispers.

"What?" She raises up to look at him. During the night one of her sleep-in contacts must have fallen out because one half of Albert is blurry and the other in focus. "Come on. Let's hear it, Albert. It's too dark for me to guess what the problem is."

"My tongue hurts."

"Your tongue?"

He starts to cry.

Albert cries like she does, tears, surely, but so quietly most of the time no one will notice.

"Hey, now." She gets out of bed and leads him into the sudden glare of the bathroom light.

"See?" He sticks his tongue in her face.

She checks the pinkness for fissures, strangenesses, God knows what she expects to find. There is nothing to report, but Albert seems comforted just to have his chin in her hand. Rose sits on the edge of the toilet while Albert perches on the footstool that used to be in Barrett's studio. She liberated it so the kid could reach the faucets. Barrett doesn't paint anymore. Those cinnamon splotches of paint ground into the wood are from another time, like cave paintings.

"Albert, I don't see anything wrong with your tongue."

"Look here. My pajamas ripped again." He holds up his right knee and sure enough, there is a neat slice right next to where Rose stitched them up. In fact, it looks as if some nimble fingers found a loose thread while certain people were attending an adults-only gallery opening.

Rose sighs. It's not the mending. Neither Albert nor Barrett know she squeaked through Home Ec with a D + . This is not what she bargained for when she made space in her closet for Barrett's things. Doesn't he realize how carefully she has to shop to avoid bringing home milk cartons with those missing children portraits? Her hip aches.

"You need to get back to sleep. School in the morning."

His freckles stand out against the pale skin. "You could tell them I have a cold." He coughs for authenticity.

"Last week we said a cold. If we do that too often, they'll ask for a doctor's note."

"Tell them I fell off my skateboard and broke my arm."

Squinting in the light, Rose imagines not the inconvenience of faking the injury, but the healing process.

"What exactly is it that bothers you about Morning Sky?"

"Miss Grace smells like old fish gravel."

"Oh, my God."

He nods, his chin quivering. "My old school had a basketball hoop. Six rabbits. I got to feed them the lunch scraps."

"It's late," she tells him. "I'm tapped for ideas. But you go tomorrow and I promise I'll talk to your dad."

He doesn't cry now, just swallows very hard and folds his hands neatly in his lap, the bare knee sticking out. When he looks at her with those clear blue eyes that have already seen what clever stories will accomplish (going home to live with his father, missing learning subtraction and stinky fish rocks) she can't help but hold out her arms. It isn't the first time she's held Albert, but it is the first time she has felt his panic paralleling her own.

She walks him to bed. No H.U.D.D.L.E. cardboard tubes for the son of Barrett Wheeler. He had Sean Lennon's bed copied from a photo and traded a carpenter studio space to build it. It is an assuming bed. There is a flexible board to jump from, a rope ladder to climb like a pirate, if Albert ever finds himself in the mood. He gets under the covers and sends her one last missile.

"There could be a cut way back where you can't see it. My mom would know where to look."

Seconds later, he's asleep, so it doesn't matter, but Rose worries anew. He's right; Sybil probably had Band-Aids that stick to things as slippery as tongues. She stuck to Barrett for six years and he is a slippery enough character. But what makes her feel powerless (besides the pain in her hip: osteoporosis? cancer? a fat ass?) is standing here at the edge of every kid's fantasy bed and realizing Albert would be more comfortable in a simple cot. She can't give him that because he is not her child. His hand curves around the adoption-papers doll she bought him that weekend in the desert, which seems an ironic note. Morning Sky's tuition costs Barrett more than his child support used to, but lacks the essentials. The basketball hoop lowered to within a successful distance, bunnies who gratefully dine on apple peelings, the clean scent of alfalfa pellets.

After ten weeks of this 'trial custody,' Albert is no more at home than he was in the desert. Yet if he were to go back to his mother, there is a part of Rose that would miss lying awake at night anticipating his visits. And out of them all — Barrett, Sybil, Albert and herself, the relationship she feels most at home with is hers and Albert's. She tries not to favor her leg on the way back to bed.

There are empty Band-Aid wrappers littering the bathroom sink. For a second, she is startled, then Barrett walks in, his face dotted with tiny wads of toilet paper and two bandages on his neck.

"Open your eyes when you shave," Rose tells him.

"I did," he says, handing her the razor. "My son and your sister used this to shave plastic off a model car. There is no such thing as a free babysitter."

Rose smiles over her toothbrush. "So where were you at three in the morning when Albert was having his attack of tongue pain?"

"It couldn't have been too dire. He managed tortilla chips for breakfast."

"Wonderful. A balanced meal. Where is he?"

"Your sister came by to borrow breakfast. Her words, not mine. You know how much Albert likes her truck. Eventually she got the hint and offered him a ride to school."

"Speaking of school. Barrett, Albert really hates Morning Sky. He says Miss Grace smells like the inside of an aquarium. I think you should talk to him."

He cups her breast. "What's to discuss? It's the best school in the district. As soon as he makes a commitment to staying, he'll cut loose."

"He's seven years old. What does he know about commitment?"

Barrett rubs his stomach. "I think I have guacamole poisoning. Get out of here so I can shit my brains out."

"I thought you did that a long time ago."

He shuts the door in her face. "I think the Lilliepad wanted you to call her."

"You never give me my messages."

* * *

Lying back down in bed she feels as isolated as that singular patch of yellow in the number twelve series canvases they sold last night. There is logic and problem-solving in Perras's work. Rose recognizes that, the salability, but it doesn't make the starkness any more likable. She moves her arms and legs, stretching the left tentatively because of her hip, trying to fill up the expanse of sheets so that the whiteness becomes the background, herself the logical subject. But at best she feels like one of the series sold out of sequence, an interruption in the progression.

Last spring, when Barrett moved in, he converted her spare room into a studio and asked her to pose. He painted parts of her into his canvases. Never her whole body, just sections interspersed with other subjects. Since they bought the gallery, he hasn't picked up a paintbrush. Since the arrival of Albert, Rose feels strange in her own house, as if someone keeps moving the furniture around.

She finds herself taking sounds as cues. Albert's midnight approaches, the intake of breath before he cries. The telephone, which may only be Lillie, but has the potential to be Sybil. The certain final click that is the door to Barrett's studio, behind which he does God knows what besides not paint. She imagines him dialoguing with the half-finished paintings, taking sides on the issue of stealing back his son.

* * *

"Barrett said you were stealing food in the kitchen again. He asked why you never eat at your own lily pad."

"Please. It's bad enough hearing that from him. Plus, it was a terrible way to start the morning. Your bread, Rose. Did you know that when you toast it the mold grows like those time-lapse sequences that scare the shit out of you on Nova?"

"I thought heat killed mold."

"Guess again."

"Bread makes you fat, Lillie. I only buy it for Albert's lunch."

"You're so naive. Kids that age never eat what you fix them. They find some Poindexter who weighs in at about one-fifty and will trade his Hostess Snowballs for carbohydrates. God, remember those sick pink marshmallow tits with the cake filling?"

"No. I ate my tuna fish on Wonder. And I'm sure Albert eats his lunch. He always brings home the empty wrappers. It proves he's not capable of deceit."

"Sounds like you researched the subject."

110

"I read it in *Your Seven-Year-Old: Friend or Foe.*"

Lillie laughs. Her laugh is great. It whoops, leaks out all over the conversation. "*Your* seven-year-old?"

"It's an impressive title."

"What's impressive is the whole situation. Rose, stuck at the impasse corral. It doesn't seem to faze you."

Rose taps the phone. "You know it does. And you know Barrett. He tells me the absolute minimum concerning Albert. I think he expects the answers to my questions to come from serendipitous living."

"Explain to me again why he wants Albert exclusively. Does Sybil beat the kid or deny him shoes?"

"No." The last thing Rose wants is the shreds of the morning to end up a ping-pong match with Lillie. They could banter for an hour and get nowhere. Lillie may be comfortable with that kind of thing, but Rose isn't. It smacks too much of dissection, flaying away at the flesh until the bones of the relationship rattle.

Lillie says, "Allow me one more observation before I hang up and go insert my foot in my mouth."

"One more little dig."

"Whatever. It's your house, Rose. Barrett moved Albert in. You have as much say as he does. Call Sybil. Get to the bottom of it."

"Goodbye, Lillie."

"Wait. The reason I called was to give you the number of that orthopedic guy. So after you call Sybil, make an appointment."

"My conscience," Rose says, "cleverly disguised as a sister."

When they hang up, Rose thinks if only things moved slowly, like that pile of lumber she kept tripping over in the hall that eventually became Albert's bed. She dials the doctor, not Sybil.

* * *

"We'll be doing a series of x-rays, so remove any jewelry,"

the nurse says. "Doctor's a fairly mellow guy, but picky as hell about this one thing."

"Even my new age crystal?" Rose says, cracking a smile.

"Oh, well. Leave it on. One never knows. Those things could turn out to be the key to the whole thing. If not, it's a nice rock."

Rose is tense. It's been years since she's had anything more than a dental x-ray. The pain in her hip seems to have disappeared, now that she's here. She holds her breath while the machine zaps away.

The examining room is full of amateur prints and curiosities. A violin bow hangs from the point. The lighted panel holding her x-rays seems to be the singular purpose-oriented piece of equipment. Lillie's orthopedic recommendation wears faded Levi's and knows Barrett.

"How's the old type-A doing? Still painting?"

"Too busy. We just bought the gallery at Sixteenth and old Newport. They say the first ten years are the hardest."

"I hope it turns out to be a successful venture for both of you. Let me study these pictures a minute."

His scrutiny is unsettling, his lack of expression more so. He doesn't look like a doctor. He could be an impostor like that man she read about in the newspaper, impersonating a gynecologist at a walk-in clinic for months. "I can't help my affliction," he'd confessed when caught. "I like women. Down there."

Barrett thought it was hysterically funny. "How can you help but sympathize with such a straightforward statement?"

"Put your own goddamn boots in the stirrups," Lillie'd said and for once Barrett was quiet.

"Do this," the doctor says, pulling Rose's leg to full extension. Her calf muscle flexes. He probes her knee, lets go.

"Well?" she asks, thinking the hip merited more than a quick feel.

"Trocanteric bursitis."

"Which means?"

"Bursa lining of joint is inflamed. I'll have the nurse give you a copy of the modified stretching exercise I recommend. But really, you have more flexibility than ninety percent of my patients."

"Should I stop exercising?"

"Not unless you relish the thought of physical therapy and cortisone injections." He makes a few notes, then looks back at her. "You could lose some weight. Every extra pound over your ideal is like four when you work out."

She flushes. Running her hand over her thigh (it isn't fat, Barrett says it's a place he can sink his teeth into) she hates this doctor's briskness. It leaves no room for asking the more unsettling questions. What if one small cell sits there malignant, too tiny to show up in pictures, but powerful, like one of those martial arts throwing stars in miniature? Don't things hurt in this achy way for a long while before someone pronounces them terminal?

"Look," he says. "I'm going to tell you something I heard the first year I started practicing. Maybe it'll help. When you hear the sound of hoofbeats, think of horses, not zebras."

She nods because adults do that instead of finishing their sentences, thinks suddenly of Albert. If she could think of a legitimate way to spring him, he would rub her hip.

* * *

"It still hurts," she says when Lillie calls.

"Maybe you sit on your ass too much."

Lillie the pink marshmallow queen, the smart sister, the lily pad who is straightforward enough to tell Barrett where he can get off when he teases her.

"What is this? Cut Rose to the bone day? The doctor as much as tells me I'm fat. Now you say I'm lazy. I sit on my ass twelve hours a day answering phones, juggling show dates and patching up fragile egos of shitty painters. Barrett and I bought this gallery together."

"So trade places for a while. That guy thinks he's God where you're concerned. Any second his beard's going to turn white and he'll issue the eleventh commandment: Rose must not leave her desk."

"You're sure making me feel better."

"Come swimming with me at the Y after God releases you from servitude. You can even bring Albert along."

"It's worth a try." But when she hangs up, Rose knows what it will be like beside her sister in the water. Lillie's laps will peel off her like skin from a tangerine, revealing a nicely sectioned fruit while Rose will end up somewhere in the deep end, floating like a goddamned dugong. Water is not her element. Running, that constant bone-jarring smack of heels on pavement is what she does best.

* * *

She calls Sybil when no one else is home.

"Yes." Sybil answers like someone asked her a simple question.

"This is Rose."

"Is there something the matter with Albert?"

"He's fine. I wondered why you never call anymore. If you wanted to arrange a visit."

Sybil laughs, a dry, flinty sound. "Let Barrett play out his hand, Rose. A few more weeks won't matter that much. Albert's coming back permanently. I think even he knows that. You must too, or you wouldn't be calling. What do you want me to say? Thank you?"

* * *

Albert is looking at the new Sears catalogue while Rose balances her checkbook. Somewhere between last month's balance and this statement, eighty dollars is running free.

"I used to circle all the things I wanted for Christmas," Rose says.

"Did you get everything?"

"Some things, sometimes the best ones. Why don't you give it a try? Have my pencil. Checkbook math is beyond my scope."

She relaxes, stretching out on the couch. Swimming with Lillie has done something because she can lie on her left side with little pain. She hovers near sleep, the scratching of Albert's pencil against the tissue-thin pages occasionally nudging her back.

"Done circling," Albert says. "Want to look?"

"In a minute."

The front door opens, shuts. Perhaps Albert is finally making friends with the kids across the way. When she hears the door again, she thinks, well at least he's trying. But the sharp smell tells her it's Barrett, sweaty from his run. She draws up her legs so he can sit beside her.

"Was ist das?"

Rose opens her eyes. "Albert circling the things he wants for Christmas from the Wish book. A great American pastime."

"Very funny."

He hands her the catalogue. The pencil bookmarks the black and white section where refrigerators and chain-link dog runs are as pale as x-rays. She starts to flip toward the toy section.

"Not there," Barrett says. "Here."

Morning Sky's reputation notwithstanding, Albert still has some distance to cover in the fine-motor department. His attempts at counter-clockwise circle closures wobble so the top connection makes it look like a little bag of money.

"So he wants a bed that looks like a truck," Rose says. "What's the harm? Look at the grillwork and the fenders. Even Lillie would like this."

"He has a bed like that back with Sybil."

Rose knows it is better to pretend to search for the missing eighty dollars in her checkbook than to say anything. She knows Barrett is going over the Sean Lennon bed in his mind, piece by piece, trying to find the error.

"It's beautifully constructed," he says. "A piece of art. Mason doweled the entire thing. There isn't one single fucking nail in it. The wood breathes."

* * *

Onion rings this time. Barrett in the dark, scattering the chemicals for cleaning her contact lenses while he searches for his bottle of Donnatol. Then he's in bed, snoring, the idea of the drug soothes him as much as the eventual effect. There is a flash of light down the hallway and Rose listens, identifying the creak of the Sean Lennon bed. Albert gets out conventionally, ignoring the uniqueness of the entrances and exits his father's bargained for him.

In the seconds before his arrival, Rose images how it will end: Lillie at the wheel of the powder-blue F-250, Albert sandwiched between them, Rose riding shotgun. They'll be teaching him the words to a Willie Nelson song instead of talking. They will have had a last swim together and be shivering against the vinyl upholstery. Sybil will be waiting with dry clothes.

THE RED HORSE

Lillie's boxy printing reads:

Jack Fletcher Junior,
No, you cannot come home yet.
Think about it. Basically,
you have two choices:

1) Buckle down and study, try
to make something of yourself
besides a chiropractor's dream.

2) Go right along jangling
your spine on bucking horses,
pickling your cerebellum in
Wild Turkey until your
cow-punching parts wear out.

Then what will you do, your bones
all sorry and mended with duct tape?

Team rope, he thinks. With the right horse, right partner, it's
a matter of correctly aiming the rope and turning the steer, leave
the fancy stuff to the heel man. There's money to be made, and
that World Team title to be won.

It is forty-eight degrees in the lobby of the men's dorm at
Central Arizona College where he has come on a rodeo scholarship. The heating system has been broken for a week after some
joker decided to steal the thermostats. Jack stands there studying

117

the Mexican paving tiles, the sneaky way they're laid crooked up by the mail slots he treks down to each day, surreptitiously (one of his vocabulary words for English 100) because he doesn't relish getting waylaid in polite conversation. This floor of the dorm houses a dozen guys like himself, hand-picked and delivered to the small junior college for their promise in sports rather than GPA'S.

As far as sports go, the only legitimate one to him is rodeo, born of skill necessary to survive in the old West, honed to an art in the new. He thought college sounded like a good deal when the coach approached him last summer in Williams.

"Get you out of the northern Arizona winter," Chance had said. Hot meals, fresh cows to yank in the dirt all year round. How's that sound, kid, compared to working the fry baskets at McDonald's when it's fifteen below? Or would you rather stare at girls in down jackets?"

But college is nothing like he expected. The classes aren't hard, but the girls are — imported from the city. For some reason he cannot quite fathom, he feels most comfortable with the handicapped girls. Their faces are soft, easy in a kind of prettiness that doesn't try so hard. The rest of them may be off, misshapen and unapproachable as cactus out back of the barn where his granddaddy used to dump motor oil, but they seem like kind girls, intelligent.

"What's your major?" he's learned to ask, having mastered those key phrases.

The brunette in the wheelchair stares him straight in the eye and answers: "Dance."

Every time. It's like trying to crack a code, he thinks.

He misses Lillie. She's back in Flagstaff, which he doesn't miss, in the nut-cracking fist of a northern storm, her rosy nipples chilling into pebbly gooseflesh as she braves the morning snowfall to grain his horse. She has a million sweet names for the animal, but to Jack, the sorrel quarter will always be nameless. It has occurred to him more than once that he left the red horse with Lillie because he's harder to remove than say, a ring from her finger.

Even though she agreed to keep the horse, she's a formidable girl to ask anything of. Nearing thirty, he thinks, but a true gentleman doesn't ask for specifics — and independent, working for a living — an engineer, no less.

Unwrapping the package that came with her letter, he fingers an expensive looking Cross pen and pencil set. There is a minute JF engraved on each, dwarfed by his big scarred hands. He guesses she expects him to work while he's here, to use up all those slivers of lead in the plastic tube, as well as write her letters. This whole business of mail is as foreign to him as his courses: Philosophy, where the professor is old enough to have been a waiter at the Lord's Last Supper; English, which required buying a dictionary that cost $16.00 — a price that seems steep for a book only full of incomplete sentences. Then there is Algebra, work-at-your-own-pace math, earn as many as ten credits. Attending class three times has already earned him five transferable units.

Yesterday, Dewaine, one of his two suitemates and a damned good potential roping partner, got a dear John from his girlfriend and went a little crazy, dismantling their dorm room furniture. He unbolted the bunk beds and tossed them into the lobby, which seemed sensible, because they were ugly, but not to the resident assistant, who came investigating the racket, threatening disciplinary action.

"Now calm down," Jack told him, "This boy's had it rough. We're gonna go rope some cows in the practice arena. Be out of your way in no time. Isn't that right, Dewaine?"

Dewaine, in a sweat and still clutching his letter, reluctantly agreed. And it wasn't bad, their times weren't the best, but three-four cows later Jack had him smiling. Ninety percent certain this could be the guy, heel man to his head, Jack was making plans. But damned if Coach Chance himself didn't show up, ordering them both off the school horses.

"What the hell you boys think you're doing? You can't ride or rope until next semester."

Jack examined the horn on his saddle, but Dewaine had words boiling inside him.

"Grounded a whole semester?"

"Unless you brought your own horse, chum."

"That some kind of blind-ass way to train for the summer circuit? What the hell are we doing here?"

"Getting an education. Now dismount."

First his girl, then the furniture, now no horses. Jack watched Dewaine heat up, only the white circle of skin around his mouth betraying him. Coach Chance saw it too.

"I can wax both your Central Arizona College boys asses, so don't even consider it."

From some place deep inside him Jack felt this telepathic urge, wishing like hell Dewaine would go on and deck the guy. But Dewaine, a third generation cowboy from Page, just spit very gentlemanly on the ground and walked away. He left the horses for Jack to untack, and by the time he'd returned to the room, Dewaine was packed and gone.

"Couldn't hack it," his remaining roommate had said. "I guess cowboys don't last around here."

"Oh, piss off," Jack told him. "You ballplayers are in the same goddamn boat and you know it."

"How's that, Tex?"

He pointed out the window to the empty campus, the north end of which was used for baseball practice. Lacking the proper water table or sufficient money, the playing diamond had been spray painted into the dirt. Jack gave his roommate's chest a patriotic thump. "Stand up, Mother. That's our National anthem they're playing."

* * *

Afternoons, in a bated silence they watch television until it's time for supper. It's all news to Jack, who missed TV growing up on a working ranch where cable didn't reach.

"The coach'll tell the professors what grades to give you," his

120

roommate promises. "Stop chewing on it. Even your worrying's loud."

Most nights they end up watching movies in the lounge till dawn; since Dewaine's exit, he hasn't found anyone he'd like as a partner, and he keeps tuning in to afternoon programs — cartoons, family shows, what he missed as a kid hauling hay, mucking out stalls.

In Algebra lab, he imagines the BRADY BUNCH, two indeterminate factors set in a common frame of reference — three blond girls, three dark boys added together to make up one family point one, wings and angles, balanced as a compass arc but for that odd housekeeper with the palm-tree hairdo somehow always changing camps. His head aches harder than the time he was shoeing the red horse and he spooked, planting one-quarter of a thousand pounds force in his thigh muscle which separated, bled internally and still pains when the weather gets like this. Perhaps it's the pounding music that blares in the dorms all hours. Everything is so foreign. What he wouldn't give for some Hank Williams, Jr. or Sr. Songs with heart. He wonders if he might be getting the flu.

* * *

Lillie's Hallmark valentine arrives, a lasso encircling a ballooning heart. It reads:

Don't ask to come home. You haven't
learned enough — I'd bet money.
Speaking of which, I hear around town
you insured the red horse. Fifteen
grand! Thanks a lot, Jack Fletcher.
I take better care of him than any
team roper would.

At lunch he thinks about how best to explain the value of a well-trained rope horse versus earning back the trust of a less than domesticated California girl when the handicapped brunette wheels over and interrupts his train of thought.

"Assuming the heaters are still busted, care for some cold spaghetti surprise?" He is determined to be friendly.

She shakes her head. "Very funny. You know we're having a dance Friday. I can't afford bloated ankles." And she curls her lip into a smile over the can of diet Coke.

"There's sodium in your drink. I read some place sodium is just as bad."

She takes a defiant gulp, sets the can down between them. "We're in the desert here, cowboy. All there is is salt and dirt."

"And dances."

She smiles. "And dances."

There's an organization for every damn thing you can think of on campus, so anything's possible. After just one mouthful, the noodles are inedible. He puts his fork down. The brunette starts to laugh, and he joins in.

"Haven't you learned anything yet? You don't dare eat to get full around here, just enough to get by."

"Someday," he says. "I'm going to catch you weepy and vulnerable. Say full moon, or first day of spring. Then we'll talk, and I'll understand what you're saying."

He trudges back to his room where his roommate is passed out in bed. His roommate's girlfriend is asleep next to him, unconscious really, but who wouldn't be after last night, mixing tequila and Seagram's and all that exercise. At home on the flat expanses of land, he's heard prairie dogs yip like that, calling out to each other shrill and biting. And an old Labrador he had to put down groaned likewise, even in his sleep. But not for that duration. Nor with that intensity, like unlubricated engine parts grinding to a desperate seizing halt. Flagstaff has snow, but he doubts it is that cold, ever. Maybe in Lillie's arms, he just doesn't feel it.

The girl is unabashed, sleeping slack-jawed on her back, her legs tangled up in sheets, her breasts exposed.

Jack stares for a while, then turns on the small color set between their beds, leaving the sound off. The BRADY BUNCH are vacationing in the Grand Canyon, which always looks better on film than it does in real life. He's hiked down those trails and never once seen that paint-by-numbers purple come from the earth. It puts him in mind of Lillie's eye makeup, that California warpaint she brought with her when she moved to Arizona (sometimes she sleeps in it), and how it was embedded in her skin that morning, reminding him of sedimentary rock. He never said so. He wanted her thrilled and remembering him in connection with seeing the GC for the first time. And she was. They'd driven out at night, slept curled in the back of his Bronco. Gently, he'd roused her at dawn to show her the canyon filling with light, the clay bowl of color coming up slow, the same way the red horse's tongue polishes his grain bucket, smart enough to savor, considering on a team roper's paycheck, it might never be that full again. There are a million things he probably should have voiced at the time, which was the right time, but he was shy of a woman that smart. Now the memory of the domestic details (mopping scrambled eggs in biscuits and gravy, Lillie's unlipsticked smile, fresh brewed coffee in that Indian diner) sends a fishhook through his heart.

He takes the silver pencil out of its case to write. Lillie wants a letter? Fine, he has a ream of notebook paper, the white surface shot through with blue lines and a thin red margin that looks like a bloodshot vein. He hasn't written a letter in maybe four years. His grandmother's dead, and to everyone else a handshake seems to suffice. After ten minutes of baffling rehearsal that leaves the paper just as blank, he licks the pencil lead and begins.

None of this Jack Fletcher Junior business,
please. I'm not at camp. No little
name tapes on my good underwear.

I've been watching a lot of old movies
on a big screen TV and heard some strange
music that would send the red horse into

one hell of a colic. That's pretty much
it.

My roommate and his girlfriend had a
letter writing contest, some deal about
about who could write the longest letter.
He wrote fifteen pages and put one stamp
on the envelope. I told him it wasn't
enough, but he said it was. He didn't
put a return address on it and it's
been in the mail ten days. That's a
baseball player for you. In my opinion
too stupid to be kept alive, let alone
go to college.

George Hubbard offered me that job in Cody as
pick-up man again. I know you don't want me
taking it. Pay's lousy, bonehead horses, and
I'll no doubt break some new bones. I'll
return the pen and pencil set if that's
what you want.

He pauses to twist the pencil lead down and looks out his
window, for the first time realizing that what's missing from the
rocky Picacho range is the softness of snow. In Lillie's bedroom,
the bay window was a picture frame for the San Francisco peaks
pillowed in white. His roommate's girlfriend wakes up, looking
out the window just in time for them both to witness the Carna-
tion truck delivering milk to the commons. The driver, a Mexican
from Yuma Jack recognizes as somebody he's rodeoed with at
one time or other, backs up and runs into the pole that feeds elec-
tricity to the dormitory. After an earthquaking thunk, he feels the
heat snap off. On the TV, THE BRADY BUNCH seal together in
a single green dot and pop out of sight, just like that, all of them
together, then gone. It feels to Jack like they've shared something

124

important, and he turns to speak, to make whatever kind of polite conversation it is a gentleman makes to a naked girl.

She sobs and tunnels back under the covers.

Is it the cold? The prospect of approaching mealtime? Losing the longest letter contest? He wants to tell her something to make it easier to stand, something he's learned, but all he can think of is *don't eat to get full, just enough to get by*, and he's afraid if he tells her that, she'll pack up and leave like Dewaine did.

He sits a minute, then borrows the keys to his roommate's new truck.

In the sand arena, he minds the coach, and ropes only goats, riding the school mascot, a nasty gray jenny who works in a hackamore. His time isn't worth spit, goats are a girl's event, but his ropes hold and the goats don't get up. Back in the truck, he cranks the engine up to 40 in reverse. He circles tighter and tighter, until the slick tires shriek into a skid, gasses the green engine, runs a stop sign going backwards and comes to rest nosed up to a dusty beige campus police car where two jugheads sit sipping coffee, just leisurely waiting for him to finish his nonsense.

The tall one licks his thumb before writing the ticket. "Let's see. Reckless driving. Illegal backing, speeding in a pedestrian zone and running a stop sign. I think twelve big ones ought to cover it."

Jack knows it will only cost him three dollars per offense because down the road there's an Indian who sells corn liquor so cheap and high in alcohol content it burns blue. These guys aren't trying to bleed him, just get a fair shake.

Neither cop says a thing about the goats in bondage on the seat beside him, or the name on the temporary registration being other than his. They chat amiably about the storm front passing east, the mare's tail clouds switching off the storm like summer flies and wait patiently while he fishes bills and change out of various pockets, trying to make twelve bucks.

* * *

With his old boots and good shirt packed into his duffel bag, Junior hoofs it across campus. He passes the brunette in the wheelchair, on her way to the library. Jogging up behind her, he grasps the armrests and gives her a spin. As her laughter fades, he hustles onto the shoulder of I-10 and points his thumb north. Palmed by the dry desert wind, every pore in his skin prickles, as tense as the paniculus muscles on the red horse, awaiting his spurred cue to leave the box. There have been hours of training, endless practice; this is his moment. He focuses only on the route in front of him, where he'll corner the cow because it's a job he does well, considering himself a little more educated with each run as he tries to narrow the distance and time between them.

MORTAR

Between the bricks at my mother's house comes a fine, red powder. Everything must have a breaking point, even mothers and daughters. Reason should support that. But the logic here escapes me. I know we're living on the fault line, but there hasn't been an earthquake. The problem is hidden, behind the wall of shore junipers when my mother first points it out.

"Come here," she says, her feet trampling the dusty miller. "Will you look at this?"

I am a good daughter. I go. I look. Just as she can't explain what prompted her to go behind the bushes, I can't tell her why it's happening. But we stand there, two women, half her gene pool motivating my behavior, the evidence clearly presented for both of us. The bricks are coming loose around the foundation at the front of the house. They're crumbling.

I toe the red dust guiltily.

"That contractor was a bigger crook than Nixon," she says.

My mother, the nouveau-liberal. "Daddy hired him," I tell her.

"Bastard," she hisses.

"Daddy?"

"Of course not. Mr. Nixon."

My mother the eternal bigot. Not that they both didn't vote the straight Republican ticket. Or that the house being seventeen years old and built of cheap materials has anything to do with brick failing. I am reminded of all those protesters fighting to save the estuaries. How on the television news coverage this one small voice carried over the room full of placards. "But isn't the natural progression of a swamp to dry up, collapse in on itself?"

I am quiet about my observations, a good daughter amid a world full of bad ones. It is a cardinal rule one learns early: never point out the obvious to your mother.

"Your father should have sued that man," she says, hands full of suckers from the dusty miller. It tends to overtake the stepping stones if you don't give it boundaries.

"Probably."

"But you know how your father was. He wouldn't sue anybody."

"I remember," I tell her, and I do. He has been dead a baker's dozen years, can't change his values now. He was embalmed, so I guess he doesn't have to worry about coming apart like defective masonry.

"Well? What do you think?" she asks, getting on my nerves with the repetition. "Is it his fault or not?"

"Probably," I answer. It is the only answer. While she clucks, spraying junipers with the hose, I stand there pondering the idea of fault. Should blame be laid crossways, so the nap shows, like in corduroy? Or just dumped at the feet, like a pile of underwear not your size?

* * *

For answers, consult an expert. The cat loves a good mystery. She is eighteen, older than the house, and has disappeared for days at a time only to return smiling. She's taken to sleeping behind the junipers in piles of the brick dust. It leaves rusty stains on her fur that flake off when she presses against my leg. The imprint makes me think of those ghostly shadows Helen Caldicott says our bodies will be reduced to if there's nuclear war. This cat follows me when I am trying to move quietly. She looks at me, deliberately knocks my shoes to the floor at two in the morning and my mother cries out in the dark:

"Who's there? Is that you?"

"Yes," I tell her, caught. "Me and the cat."

The cat knows too much, like a character out of a Stephen

King story. She's part of a childhood I keep insisting I've grown out of, have no need to remember. Except as she continues to age, I see time reverse itself, and I'm this scrawny redhead crying against the calico, sneezing afterwards.

Right now she's playing innocent, sleeping in a bed of lobelia among the shredded bark she tore from the white birches. Only a papery strip on her claws gives her away. My mother planted them, a stand of four, after she saw a cover of *Sunset* magazine. One died immediately. The remaining three are puny, but tall. A good wind could tear them from the earth, but not a cat and surely not bricks.

I see more in this animal than a glimpse of myself as a ten-year-old, petting the eight-ball skull. Rescued from the trash while she was still wet, that worm of umbilicus still viable, she was never a liar. She showed her need from the start, clawing eyedroppers of milk from my hand.

My father would say "That cat's got to go," as if she were a threat. He never quite cottoned to her as a pet. Which caused me blindly to defend her and the cat grew up knowing it. Even now, her awareness is inherent in her actions. When the newspaper boy's wrist flicks the daily, she straightens so that it just misses her.

"How can you trust anyone who has it in for cats?" my mother cries.

"You can't," I tell her. You can hardly trust anybody.

Trust involves a leap of faith; you have to think about Fill in the missing letters, like *Wheel of Fortune*. This is a cat who would sell aluminum cans to get enough coin to bribe the paper boy to do it again. Extra tuna in the dish. Half-and-half when water would do. This is a cat who knows exactly what is wrong with the bricks, but is not telling.

But I wonder, am I any different, lying all these years, sneaking my lovers into the house? I kneel on what's left of dancer's knees, ruined by leaps I had no business making. I know it appears as some leftover ritual from a Catholic childhood. I finger the dust from the disintegrating brick. It does not seem as simple as clay dust. There is a sinister, carcinogenic, red dye number two feel to it. Red, like I chose for every favor candy. Red like cat's eyes in the dark. Red like the time my father tore from me that tympan of flesh that was supposed to be private, sacred, mine. Red like the hard words from my mother's lips when she doubted me. Red is a color that stays with me, bitterly, forever, solid as bricks.

Think: I should be more grown up about this. It's only water and earth, for Christ's sake. Forgive, forget, get up and dance in a different direction. Be a cat.

But even as the thoughts formulate, I see myself and know I'll never be free of the past. I'm not beyond turning leaves on the trees inside out, claiming rain is imminent, or picking the seed pods from the birches, rubbing them to confetti. I haven't moved much beyond those kitten years of sucking Jell-o through the space between my front teeth, ignoring the stain it made down the center of my tongue, dark as deceit.

* * *

My lover says he doesn't have any idea why the bricks would fall apart, why the red dust. He says he cares only for my body as it is now; nothing else matters. But I know he senses the wall in me. You can't ignore something like this. It comes out of the cracks, leaving empty spaces, it seeps onto the sheets like truth.

Those moments he puts his hand up to shield my eyes, I lay there under the shadow of his fingers, wondering if he can't bear to look either. The occasional agonies are part of the mystery, aren't they? When he pushes too deep and it feels like he nicks my womb, I no longer do anything to stifle my cries. There is the almost familiar ache in my wrists as he holds me down; what works taught early returns. But I do not complain or mistake aching for passion. I am the one with the questionable needs, it seems, examining bricks.

When I ask, he says he has no qualms about suing, should the action seem appropriate. When I let him spend the night, I make him read me to sleep. If I find the red dust on the pillow, I shut my eyes and listen. His voice is redwood deep, steady as rain through birches. All that other business disappears on the periphery of vision.

If it weren't so comfortable, if it didn't seem so fragile, I would wake my mother, because finally I think I know some answers as to why brick fails to hold up under years of deceit. It's a cat's logic, not a cause, never that, but kind of a complement to the color red. This is what everyone needs between their bricks. It seems essential, like mortar.

THE RINGS OF SATURN

"Space is what matters," I told my son, pricing his battered fire truck at two dollars. Christmas was barely two months away and my husband Ross hadn't been working much because of the rainy season. The extra money from the garage sale would pay some bills, tuck a few surprises into the stockings.

Ross says two things are perfect reflections of my personality — my oversized shoulder bag, which doubles as library, pharmacy and portable cafeteria — and the garage. I've looked around. The shoulder bag seems standard for women my age. On the surface we may appear to have sold out our sixties idealism in favor of the ordinary miracles — having babies, mortgages in suburbia, but Ross teases about it going deeper, as if some part of me still carts the essentials, ready to depart at a moment's notice.

The garage held everything but the car. My old term papers on Hopi pottery, a series of blue jeans ranging from size 3 to size 11, when I wore them defiantly, a safety-pin over my expanding belly, unable to accept the idea of a stretchy maternity panel as a reflection of me, even the temporarily pregnant me.

I shook out the jeans (I'll never be a size 3 again), marked them fifty cents a pair. The textbooks could go, too, a quarter apiece? But not my art books, whose only flaw is that they are too tall for the bookshelves. Those would stay. I pieced together the second-hand crib Jason slept in seven years ago. The lamb decals were chipped and curling. It gave me pause, but I knew in my heart there wouldn't be any more babies. I marked it ten dollars and set it up on the lawn.

Under two cracked tarps Ross and I once strung together for

a camping tent, I found the saddle my father gave me for Christmas the year I turned eleven.

The tobacco-colored leather was in remarkably good shape for having been ignored. I fingered the child-sized stirrups and couldn't believe my feet were ever so small. The silver concha had tarnished a dull green. From an assortment of cleaners Ross had stacked on the shelves, I picked one for silver. I rubbed with a corner of my t-shirt until the engraving surfaced. The scalloped edges glinted in the early morning sun. I turned the silver discs this way and that, letting them catch and throw light. They flashed in my eyes. It was deliberate, even painful, and despite the passage of thirty Christmases, I realized this was a place that had never quite healed.

I was ten. My sister Sallie was five months old and smelled like the cafeteria at my elementary school. I gave her a bath, but it hadn't helped much. I dressed her in a ruffly pinafore that belonged to Baby Elaine, my biggest doll. Sallie's legs felt cold, so I pulled red tights on her. I wished for just this once, she would lie as still as my doll, so there wouldn't be any chance of her getting dirty. I put her in the playpen with a stuffed animal. Right away, she drooled down the front of the dress.

My mother was in the bathroom soaking her feet in a basin of hot water. She had just gotten off work. Her cheeks were flushed, she looked tired and cranky.

But my father was coming. When the sky turned blue-black, dark enough to find the Little Dipper easily, he would be here, smelling of the horses he broke for a living, bringing the best present of all. Himself.

I lit all the candles so that he couldn't lose his way. The Santa one from Woolworth's cost seventy-five cents, new, saved out of my lunch money. The bayberry pair we kept from last year were half-burned down, but once they were lit, he'd never know.

The apartment had no fireplace, but the room felt as warm as if there were one, lined in smooth rocks, burning orangewood. The chicken I put in to roast had crisp skin, just the way he liked it. He would sit down to eat, smile and never want to leave us again.

It was Christmas eve, the longest night of the year. The air outside was so different, so quiet, that I wondered, even though we lived in the desert, if it just might snow.

Dinner was long over before I heard that tentative knock at the door. The chicken sat dried out on the counter, forgotten. Sallie had fallen asleep. But as I watched from the hallway, my mother's face slipped from a frown to a barely concealed joy.

It was one of his iron-clad rules; no one could be unhappy when he came.

We played all the records we owned, twice. The candles puddled down. Sallie fell asleep again and I held my eyes open with my fingers, listening to his stories — cattle brandings, a spotted mare that gave birth to twins, secret Indian ceremonies that involved eagle's feathers and blood.

Then he stopped talking. They looked at each other and kissed. Long, slow kisses that made me like scary Indian stories better. Their glasses made circles on the coffee table, hers going around his, like Saturn and that ring that follows it everywhere that I studied in school.

I reminded them it was Christmas eve, that Santa was supposed to fill those stockings with something. They smiled at me, laughed, poured more wine into the fancy red glasses he'd won last summer at the county fair.

Who could sleep on Christmas Eve? It felt more like racing with angels, a glittery drifting in and out of dreams, thinking I heard voices, waking to sounds that might be Sallie fussing, but were gone when I listened. Later I heard clearly. I sat up in bed and held onto my sister until the curtains were tinted amber with dawn.

"Don't crowd me, damn it!"

"But you promised. This time you promised."

Boot heels on stairs. Door slamming. The way my mother cried. A Christmas carol on the radio.

The unmistakable scent of new leather wafted up the stairwell and I could picture the saddle. All my life I had wanted nothing else. I'd smiled and said thank you for dolls and musical jewelry boxes, but somehow he knew what I needed. That I would someday be a rider like him, living my life outdoors, charting my path by the stars. I vowed I'd be different.

I sold the jeans to the girl who occasionally babysat Jason. She couldn't get over the bell bottoms, like "bat wings," she told me. I saw a Mexican couple admire the crib. They counted their money and turned away. Then the woman looked back, not yet willing to give up hope and I marked the crib down to seven-fifty so they could afford it. Jason hung onto his fire truck, defiantly hiding the price tag whenever anyone expressed interest.

When a real estate lady placing flags for an open house stopped her station wagon and moved toward the saddle, invisible hackles rose on my back.

"I don't see a sticker," she said. "How much are you asking?"

"I'm not sure. I guess you could make me an offer."

"Western decor is so popular," she told me. "With a little decorative paint, this could be a real conversation piece." She offered me two hundred dollars. "More than it's worth," she reminded me.

Jason looked at me. It was more money than he could imagine. Ross had an expression, too. We could pay for Christmas without dipping into the savings. The real estate lady tapped the toe of her Anne Klein pump in my asphalt driveway, four hundred miles from where I grew up scuffing dirt, one eye always on the horizon, waiting for that man to come down off the mountain and need me like he did his cowboying.

She scribbled on a card. "Here's my home phone number. Call me when you change your mind."

Ross and I took twenty dollars from the garage sale and decided on a night at the movies. We let Jason choose which one. He settled on a John Wayne festival at the Odeon. We could stay till midnight if we felt so inclined. In the dark, I watched him more than the movie. His profile is less like Ross than it is like my father. There's a ridge to his brow, a stubborn bump, he would have called it, if he'd stuck around long enough to see my child.

Ross touched my hand in the dark and even without his kiss or a declaration, I knew there was love here, as tangible and permanent as the words etched inside my wedding ring. But he was right, about my purse, about the garage. As much as I try to deny it, sometimes I have the urge to go, not to any place other than here, exactly, but somewhere uncharted.

On the screen, John Wayne galloped his horse toward anonymous mountains. It was night; the only light to go by came from stars, each one shining down hard from its proper place. A falling star streaked light across the land, momentarily revealing the narrow passage for the trail. Maybe it was a special effect, or maybe the director had just gotten lucky. Up above us the ceiling of the aging theater sported a few dying stars itself — fluorescent paint from the time when this kind of darkness held magic. The projectionist would click on the cloud machine and for a few hours I could believe the universe was compact, traversable and that my father would be coming back.

I remembered how he once had me hold the reins of his horse — how all that rangy muscle stood ready and that I had to struggle to believe leather alone would keep him grounded — one of a dozen times I'd taken him at his word, scarred, but steady in the orbit of daughterly love. Now, with my free hand I reached in my pocket and crumpled the real estate woman's business card. I rejoined hands with Ross, and then Jason. Staring up at the *faux* stars, I resumed my search for Saturn, certain if I looked hard enough, someday I would find it.

STATISTICS

I was outside, watering violets that had travelled from my mother's flower bed on the east coast — twisted roots she'd wrapped in damp paper towels and hidden in her purse for the plane trip — when I witnessed the exchange.

"Ben Harper, you let that bird alone," Mrs. Carmody hissed. "God never meant for all His creatures to survive."

My ten-year-old ignored her.

"Mark my words! You'll catch a disease!" she hollered after him, waving the dustpan she had been trying to scoop the bird into.

Every neighborhood has one. In my childhood, it was Mr. Cruikshank, who honed my rollerskating skills to a critical edge by spreading sand on the sidewalk in front of his house. He had a twelve-gauge he was fond of using on displaced wildlife. I'd seen baby skunks and oppossum murdered so often Cruikshank became a key figure in my nightmares. I'd vowed to get even, but as time passed, the opportunity never seemed to arise. I set the hose down and called Ben over.

He was out of breath with excitement. "What kind of bird is it, Mom? Can I keep him?"

The beginnings of no-color feathers poked up from the gray skin. One eye blinked weakly. It was a hatchling, fallen from the nest.

"It probably won't live till morning," I told him brusquely. "The best we can do is make him a soft place to be comfortable."

His eyes filled.

"Look, Ben. I tried this dozens of times when I was your age. He's awfully tiny. Let's just take it one step at a time."

"And hope for the best, right?"

"Sure. I guess we can do that."

Ben sacrificed his bed pillow and a beach towel so faded the pattern was discernible only through memory. He hovered over the box all afternoon, taking time out only for supper. He tried an eye dropper full of cereal, a freshly dug worm from the garden. I knew the squaring of my ten-year-old's shoulders. How a child's will is interwoven with fancy, but is a will, nonetheless. He was as obstinate as his father, as if genes carry that quality, too. I was amazed. It seemed because he believed it so that the bird lived to see the morning.

I gave birth to Ben before it was fashionable again to be having babies. Took him for walks in a cheap stroller, nothing like the Cadillacs available these days. I wore gingham maternity tops studded with rickrack, because that was all I could find. I ate what I pleased, took a gamut of pills for my blood pressure. The doctor said it was all right; now he might say differently. All around me I see pregnant women living as pure as monks. They have amniocentesis performed as casually as my mother hung my wedding band suspended by sewing thread over my belly to discover the sex of her first grandchild.

"Boy," she proclaimed, though the doctor, citing heartbeats and averages, was talking girl the whole nine months.

"Nobody's perfect," Ben's father told me then, tells me now, again and again. "Everyone has something wrong with them. Look around you. You'll see."

I knew this lecture. The man with no shoes versus the man with no feet. That kind of rationalizing used to make me feel even guiltier. Now I thought it was like trying to sound a brass gong using a feather. Futile to try, but oh, that weight's still there. Heavy and silent, it hung in my gut, an unsung alarm. I figured when the bird died, under the peach tree would be the best place to bury it.

The next morning he was still cheeping, demanding food. I drove to the pet shop and for $8.50 purchased a gummy sack of grain to be mixed with precisely 98-degree water and fed every three hours. *Fill the craw*, it said, *but don't overfill*. No illustrations to guide me. It was probably a waste of money. I told Ben he'd have to help with the feedings and he was enthusiastic, but I knew all the while that at three A.M., I'd end up doing this alone.

How hungry he was at the first feeding. All beak, stubs of wings scrabbling against the sides of the shoebox. He managed Ben's syringe full of formula and collapsed exhausted in a heap, smeared bony down, that worn towel for a nest.

"Did I kill him?" Ben wanted to know.

I took his hand and gently placed it against the sopping breast. His eyes grew wide.

"I can feel his heart, Mom. It's banging like anything."

It's those invisible lines that inevitably trip you, the connection from heart to heart, as Ben's fingertips pulsed his less-than-perfect blood through his veins. Touch was touch. It made no difference who to the bird. Even substitute mother-love couldn't be damned up, allowed to flood only to a certain boundary. Ben grinned down at the bird. I had to admit, it was tougher than I expected. I remembered Statistics, the course I had to take in order to graduate from college.

Ben's transfusions. Before 1983, when they began screening blood. Nine years had passed. He showed none of the symptoms. On the surface, everything seemed fine. But. Lately, this had become my preoccupation. Daily, before rising, I prayed to be among the lucky percentages from those terrifying initials that spelled a grim future for so many. I scoured the newspapers for data. Facts flowed through my consciousness and tried to make them lie down into a graph, reasonable information. I had heard there was a test now. But even with better odds than the bird, I couldn't quite bring myself to have it performed.

I've known more than my share of doctors. They will sit there and tell you the heart is just a muscle, operating automatically on impulses from the brain. But I felt certain mine secreted dark chambers whose contents were more frightening than what you'd find in a haunted house.

Ben's voice startled me. "What are you thinking about, Mom?"

I answered quickly. "How big you're growing."

Satisfied, Ben went outside to play. With a cotton swab, I carefully wiped the bird's beak, blotting out everything but the task before me.

In bed that night, my husband sighed and pulled me close, secure even in his dreams. I wasn't sleeping; I told myself I was just a little keyed up, but really I was listening for the bird.

Nestled in my husband's arms, I listened to the sound of his breathing, clean and deep. I imagined roots flowing out from the soles of his feet, ever widening, sending down an infinite number of tap roots. That should have relaxed me, but instead I woke him.

"What is it?"

I tried to keep the tears out of my voice. "What it always is."

"I keep telling you, it's been too long. If the blood had been infected, surely something would have shown up by now."

"I know you're right." I tapped my chest. "But in here."

"In there what?"

"In here I don't know anything at all."

He propped himself on one elbow and looked at me. "There's a simple way to tell."

"Have the test done. But what if..."

He pressed his finger to my lips. "Shh. It won't. He's fine. I'll take care of it if you want."

Even he knew it wasn't the kind of offer that required a response. Mothers do these tasks. For his dad to suddenly take time off work to accompany him to the doctor would alert Ben to the immensity of what was happening. There would be questions he would want answered. If it were to be done at all, I would have to be the one to instigate it. A smile locked on my face, every hair in place, calmness exuding from me like ripples in a lake.

My husband fell back to sleep.

Dried formula caused the bird to lose feathers in patches. He looked frightful as he craned his neck to ask for more. Ben had come early, too, slipping out of me as easily as a puppy. He held his own for a week, and the doctors were hopeful, then he back-slid so far he needed surgery, which necessitated the blood trans-

142

fusions. I remember watching him from outside the nursery, those scrawny limbs hooked up to tubes and monitors. I held onto my mother's arm for support. From a clear plastic bag, the blood flowed into him, dark as grape jelly. It scared me so badly that for the first time I understood the term weak-in-the-knees. My mother never wavered.

"Because of that blood," she told me, "he came back to us."

She was right. When the nursery rang out with his cry, when he cracked his first smile and forever charmed two student nurses, my mother was right and it was good.

As I replaced the soiled towel beneath him, the bird wrapped his claws around my fingers and held on. He hung there for a moment, then lost his balance.

"Time to tell old lady Carmody she was wrong," my husband said when I told him.

"She may prove to be right yet," I said. "Somehow he has to learn to fly."

He winked. "It can't be that hard. You taught me."

Gawky head, too big for his body, how impossible flight seemed. What incredibly hard work. Ben's story books made it sound heavenly. Even the smallest animal characters soared high above the planet until the earth reduced to a manageable piecemeal. To them, flight was a verb, the last resort, the only escape from whatever stalked you. To me it was nothing short of a miracle. Aerodynamics had nothing to do with it. I knew what held up the passenger jets that passed over our house when fog drove them to alternate routes: the collective will of mothers.

He was clinging to the curtain when I returned from the pet shop with a styrofoam cup of mealworms — wild-eyed at the window and what lay beyond. It would have taken me a few steps to reach it, undo the latch and push the screen down. Outside, the pomegranate bush was in bloom; fruits I'd seen other birds feed on would soon follow. But I cupped my palm and captured him instead, returning him to the crude cage I'd fashioned, an old aquarium with a chicken wire lid.

He grew fat on the worms. He ate however many I placed in front of him, and slept.

"But everybody's been except me!" Ben wailed, waving the goldenrod flyer for summer camp. "Even Stevie Brewster and he's only six. Why can't I go?"

"Maybe next year."

He stamped his foot. "You always say that!"

"You'd get homesick. What about your bird?"

A week in the mountains. Boys played rough. In the name of friendship, I'd seen them wrestle to the ground, blacken each other's eyes, and in the kind of blind camaraderie that will never come again, nick fingertips to become blood brothers.

Ben's glare belonged on Mt. Rushmore. "I bet Dad would've said yes."

The screen door slammed and he was gone. Our voices woke the bird and he cheeped and trilled, using shrill tones that alarmed me. It took me a full minute before I recognized the vocalizations for what they were: the first attempts at birdsong.

I had kept him a day too long. Ben had provided me with the opportunity to right that childhood injustice I'd always hoped to; I'd proved the Mrs. Carmody's of the world wrong. Now, if I didn't let go, I would be just as bad as they were. Before I could lose my courage, I took the aquarium outside and set it on the picnic table. I lowered my finger and the bird hopped up, cocking its head as if to test the air. Then after three short hops, he flew into a silver maple.

Where my mother lives, their leaves turn brittle and crumble in the bitter winter cold, yet they come back, managing to grow into sturdy giants, surviving generations. Long after the bird had flown away, I stood there, holding one of the leaves. I studied the careful symmetry. On the underside, the veins traveled unbroken to the stem. Dumping the mealworms into a plate, I left it tucked into a V of branches, just in case the bird got hungry. Then I went inside to call Ben's doctor, because going to camp required a complete physical.